Moonlight, coupled with longing and loneliness, did strange things to people, Tyler thought.

The moon was the loneliest of the heavenly bodies. He could feel its pull right now. Could feel, too, the pull of the woman standing before him.

For the past nine months he'd lived every day with an emptiness he hadn't known what to do with. Tonight, for a small amount of time, he'd forgotten about that emptiness. Forgotten because Brooke's words had somehow filled it. Her words, her laughter.

Her.

Had he thought it through, he wouldn't have done it. But he wasn't thinking. He was reacting.

As if hypnotized, Tyler lowered his head and touched his lips to hers, kissing Brooke very, very slowly. Just the way his heart was suddenly beating.

For the first time in nine months, he felt alive.

Dear Reader,

Welcome to Silhouette Special Edition, to a world full of life, love and family.

Allison Leigh effortlessly picks up the baton in THE STOCKWELLS family books with *Her Unforgettable Fiancé*, where proximity provokes passion in a couple who should have married years ago. And there's another couple who should have become a couple a long time ago, but when they do get together it's really special—look for *At the Heart's Command* by Patricia McLinn, which has another linked book coming next month, too.

Marie Ferrarella returns once more with a touching book about a father who's given up everything to keep his three daughters safe, *Father Most Wanted*, and if you're a fan of Marie's you'll be delighted to know that she has a new book next month also. There's another dad in Suzanne Carey's *When Love Walks In*, but the twist is that he doesn't know he has a son.

Susan Mallery's *Wife in Disguise* is the last of her LONE STAR CANYON books where an accident makes Josie Scott rethink what's important to her—her sexy ex-husband. And finally our THAT'S MY BABY! title is a little different this month even though it still has a cute baby in it; do let us know what you think of *A Bundle of Miracles* from Amy Frazier.

Enjoy them all.

The Editors

Father Most Wanted
MARIE FERRARELLA

SILHOUETTE®
SPECIAL EDITION™

Silhouette, Silhouette Special Edition and Colophon are registered trademarks of Harlequin Books S.A., used under licence.

*First published in Great Britain 2002
Silhouette Books, Eton House, 18-24 Paradise Road,
Richmond, Surrey TW9 1SR*

© Marie Rydzynski-Ferrarella 2000

ISBN 0 373 24346 4

23-0302

*Printed and bound in Spain
by Litografia Rosés S.A., Barcelona*

This one's for
April,
who always makes me
smile

Chapter One

"Ow."

Brooke Carmichael pressed her lips together, sealing in any further sounds. The tips of her fingers where the hot espresso had sloshed over the side of the coffee container pulsed with pain. That's what she got for not waiting for a cover, she thought.

Still hurrying, her eyes now riveted to the guilty container, she switched hands and shook the excess moisture off her fingers. The barely-out-of-puberty boy who was single-handedly manning Coffee Heaven's counter had told her he was all out of lids, but there were some in the back.

Since he moved with the speed of a snail, his finding one didn't sound like a feat that was going to be accomplished any time within the next half hour. Brooke didn't have a half hour. She didn't even have five extra minutes to spare. Since Heather had called saying she'd be late, there was no one to watch Tell Me a Story, the bookstore Brooke had owned for the past two years.

Ordinarily when Isaac, the regular clerk, was behind the trendy coffee-shop counter, the whole transaction took less than two minutes. But Isaac had been nowhere in sight and there was no way Brooke could begin the day without molten sludge oozing through her veins, waking her up. The coffee she'd had at home only got her as far as the store and no farther. She needed something guaranteed to jump-start narcoleptics before she could begin her workday.

Her sister *would* pick today to be late. "When it rains, it pours," Brooke muttered to herself.

Next time she'd bring a thermos, the way she used to when she'd been the only one tending to the bookstore. Having help had made her lax. She blew on fingers that still stung.

"Tiffany, where are you?" a male voice called.

Intent on not spilling her espresso again, Brooke didn't see the tall, somber-looking man until it was almost too late. Coming to an abrupt halt, she barely avoided launching the contents of her container at him.

Her heart hammering, the fingers of her left hand christened in the exact same manner as the ones on her right and now smarting, Brooke narrowly avoided what could have been a very nasty accident.

Stepping back and to the side, Brooke realized that the man was not alone. He was flanked by matching bookends in the form of two identical little girls, no more than about five or six. Their dresses were similar, if not exactly the same, but one face was as close to a mirror image of the other as anything Brooke had ever seen. The man was holding their hands tightly and seemed to look through Brooke as if she wasn't there.

Brooke's gaze dropped to the twins again. What must it be like, she wondered, to know there was someone else walking around with a face exactly like yours? It might make an interesting children's-book series. Something her father would have deftly written about, she thought with a bittersweet pang.

"Sorry," she apologized when she caught her breath.

Oblivious to the near collision, the man hardly spared her a look. He seemed far more intent on finding this Tiffany person. Then, nodding vaguely in Brooke's direction, as if the apology had replayed itself in his head, he hurried past her, the two little girls held fast in tow.

"Tiffany," he called.

"No harm done, I guess," Brooke murmured to herself, heading out into the mall.

The man no doubt had misplaced his wife, Brooke mused. He had that father-on-an-outing harried look. Turning back, she squinted, looking intently at the hand that held on to the little girl on his left. There it was, a wedding ring.

Had to be the wife, she decided.

Why were all the gorgeous ones taken? she wondered.

Not that she would be interested in the man one way or the other, she amended, entering her store. She was doing just fine the way she was, carving out her own business and her own niche in the world. At twenty-seven, she figured she was way overdue in both departments. She'd put in her time on the marriage-go-round and all it had done was make her dizzy—and incredibly cynical.

There was a time, she thought as she paused to straighten a display of books dealing with the adventures of a timid ladybug, when she would have said that there wasn't a cynical bone in her body. But that was before Marc. Her ex-husband had done that to her, siphoned off her optimistic view of life and made her cynical.

Marc, with his dark good looks and his secret roving eye. Brooke sighed and shook her head, then took a long sip of her coffee.

Nope, she wasn't going to spoil a perfectly lovely morning by thinking about the one dark spot in her life. The two-year-old divorce decree had physically removed Marc from her life; now it was up to her to eradicate all traces of him from her mind.

Taking another long sip of coffee, Brooke closed her eyes and waited for the double espresso's effect to kick in. It didn't take long. She blew out a breath. "Well, that'll sure get you going in the morning," she murmured.

As a rule, mornings in the mall were slow. Customers didn't begin coming into Tell Me a Story until around noon or later. That was okay with her. Right now, Brooke decided, she could use a little alone time. She was comfortable with her own company. Always had been.

After a third sip, Brooke looked at the dwindling contents of her cup thoughtfully. There was a new trend taking hold amid the chain bookstores. She supposed she could go that route and start selling beverages. At least it would cut down on her making quick dashes to Coffee Heaven.

The next moment, the idea faded. Most of her customers were under four feet in height and tended to have sticky hands to begin with. Given her clientele, to provide only coffee was ridiculous. To provide punch and juice, instead, would be far from practical unless she began dealing in books with plastic-coated washable pages.

She thought of the man she'd almost bumped into. Maybe packets of vitamins for harried parents would be a better sale item. Something to help them keep up with their energetic offspring.

A smile curved Brooke's mouth as her thoughts drifted to the past. She could remember her father commenting on that more than once. That he needed megavitamins just to keep up with her and Heather.

But that, she thought, was because Jonathan Carmichael had tried to do it all, be both mother and father to Brooke and her sister while he worked full-time at writing and illustrating children's books. Her smile widened. He'd done a fair job of it, too. Not so much as a day ever went by when she and Heather didn't feel loved. Most of the time, her father made juggling a million things look easy, but there were times, she knew, that it got to him. He tried not to show it, but she knew nonetheless. She was the older one and intuitive.

Now that she thought about it, the man she'd almost succeeded in dousing with coffee had that exact same harried look in his eyes.

She hoped he'd found his wife by now.

Sufficiently fortified with caffeine, Brooke threw the empty container into the wastebasket behind her cash register, then squared her shoulders. That new shipment of books in the back wasn't going to unpack itself.

Making her way to the rear of the store and the storage room that also doubled as her office, Brooke stopped and sucked in her breath. She could have sworn she was alone, but there on the floor, making herself right at home, was one of the girls that man had had in tow just minutes ago. She'd obviously gotten away from him.

That was going to have to be fixed.

"Hi there," Brooke said.

Large blue eyes, fringed with long black lashes, looked up at her before they returned to the books that populated the bottom shelf. "Hi."

Brooke squatted down to the little girl's level. Her young unchaperoned customer seemed to be scrutinizing the different titles on the book spines. Could she read them, Brooke wondered, or was she just pretending? Her own father had taught her and Heather to read at such an early age Brooke felt as if she'd been born reading. Maybe the girl's parents had done the same for her and her twin.

In either case, Brooke knew that the last thing a child welcomed was a condescending adult. She knew she never had. She spoke to her the way she would to any adult. "May I help you find something?"

There was no shyness about the child. Instead, she seemed filled with purpose, a mission, and poise beyond her years. She nodded smartly before answering. "Yes, do you have any books about mommies?"

"I might. What kind of book did you have in mind?"

The girl hesitated, as if trying to find the right way to phrase what she was about to say. "One about finding one."

Wasn't that cute? She was trying to help her father find her mother by turning to a book for guidance. Whoever said reading was dead? Brooke nodded as if giving the choice serious consideration. "So, you're looking for your mommy?"

The blue eyes took on a sparkle as the little girl looked up at her. "Yes. We all are."

All. That would be her father and her sister, Brooke guessed. Ordinarily she would have led the girl to several books dealing with mothers. There was one about a lost bear cub Brooke particularly liked.

But the way she saw it, she had a far more pressing service to perform. "Well, right now, I think your daddy is going out of his mind trying to find both of you."

The girl frowned thoughtfully, as if she didn't quite follow that. "You know my daddy?"

"I don't exactly know him," Brooke confessed, trying to be strictly honest. Kids, she knew, respected and expected honesty. "But I do know what he looks like." Brooke leaned her head in closer to the little girl, lowering her voice as if to share a secret with her. "Worried."

There was a light in the blue eyes, as if a connection had just been made. The little girl nodded with enthusiasm. "Yes, he does. He looks like that all the time now." She turned her face up and frowned sadly. "Do you have any books to help?"

"No, but I think that taking you to him might help. A lot." The poor man was already looking for his wife. Having to look for this little girl, as well, wasn't exactly going to put him in a better frame of mind. Brooke stood up and took the little girl's hand gently, drawing her to her feet. "What do you say we go look for him?"

It wasn't unusual to have children wander into her shop. After all, she'd gone to great lengths to make it pleasing to the young eye. There were carefully painted murals depicting cartoon characters and fairy-tale folks either sitting, standing or comfortably sprawled out, their hands tucked around a good book. Blessed with her father's gift for illustration, it had taken Brooke weeks to do, and she had purposely made it into an inviting peaceful version of Wonderland—if Wonderland had been a place where books were offered, instead of mind-confounding puzzles.

But usually any child who wandered in was soon followed by a parent or two. A parent who was happy to have a few minutes respite from the taxing job of parenting.

Brooke glanced toward the entrance. Mr. Drop-Dead Gorgeous with the worried frown was nowhere in sight. Not a good sign. She hoped he hadn't gone off to the opposite end of the mall.

The little girl appeared undecided about whether or not to follow Brooke. Two large front teeth flanked by far smaller baby ones nibbled on her lower lip as she thought it over.

"Okay," she finally agreed. "Daddy says we shouldn't talk to strangers, but I guess you're okay."

Flattered, Brooke paused to make things clear. "Thank you, honey, but your daddy is right, you know. You shouldn't talk to strangers."

Walking out of the store, she drew the girl to her side and paused to press a button on the inside wall. A decorative gate, fashioned to look like the twining ivy that had grown around Sleeping Beauty's castle while she took her extended nap, descended slowly into place. Brooke flipped a latch, locking it. Finding the little girl's missing father could just possibly take longer than dashing out for a cup of espresso, and she couldn't afford to have any more customers come wandering in. The way she saw it, she'd used up her luck with this one. The next pint-size customer might innocently or not so innocently make off with several books.

The little girl was still mulling over the warning she had just received. Confused, she looked up at Brooke. "Then I shouldn't talk to you?"

Brooke looked around, trying to spot the man and his solitary daughter. She glanced at the girl's face next to her. "I see we have a conundrum."

The girl's eyes widened. "We do? What's a con—a ca—?"

"Conundrum," Brooke repeated, grinning. "That means a tricky puzzle—like the one we're in right now. You shouldn't talk to strangers, which ordinarily would mean me, but you have to talk to someone because if you don't, your daddy might not be able to find you. And I'm sure that would make him very sad."

"He's already very sad. Daddy's been sad for a long time now," the girl confided, then paused, thinking. Her eyes brightened as she looked up at Brooke. "If you tell me your name, then you won't be a stranger anymore."

There was a sweet innocence in the little girl's thinking that touched Brooke. In this fast-paced world with its predators, things weren't nearly that simple anymore. But right now, an explanation would only confuse things further, and time was probably of the essence.

"My name's Brooke," she told her.

The little girl cocked her head. "Like where water runs?"

Brooke laughed. "I guess that's one way to describe it. Okay, now that you know who I am, let's go see if we can find your dad."

The smile went beyond cooperative straight to beatific. "Okay."

A darkness closed around his heart. He knew that he was letting his mind get carried away, but nine months ago, he would never have dreamed that Gina's life would be taken right before his eyes. Things like that only happened in the kinds of movies he didn't care to watch.

As did kidnappings.

Even the hint of the word caused sharp chills to tingle their way down his spine. But what else could have happened? His daughter knew better than to wander off.

He'd only looked away for a second. But a second was all it took for something bad to happen.

He couldn't think like that, he admonished himself. It would drive him crazy. And then where would the girls be?

"We'll find her, Daddy," Bethany told him. She sounded so much older than her years. Almost as if she were the parent and he the child.

Ironic humor tugged at his soul. "I'm supposed to be the one saying that to you."

"Oh. Sorry."

"You don't have anything to be sorry about. Ever," he told her, toning down the fierceness in his voice. "Your sister, when we find her, however, does." He looked down at the little girl on his left. "Are you sure she didn't say where she was going?"

The girl shook her head, her dark curls bouncing like tiny springs. "She was just gone."

Gone. The word echoed in his mind. No, he refused to let himself go there, refused to entertain any idea except that he would find her. He *had* to.

"Look, Daddy, over there!" Excitedly Bethany pointed beyond the carousel at the same moment she began tugging on her father's arm. "There she is, with some lady."

His heart iced over, the words registering before he had the opportunity to see for himself. He turned his steps in the direction Bethany was tugging, hurrying before he even looked at the terrain. He zigged around the heavyset security guard just in time. The older man looked at him oddly as he made his way to his daughter.

Good. Keep watching. Maybe we'll need you.

But the instant he saw his wayward daughter, he knew he'd just allowed himself to overreact. Instinct told him everything was all right. His daughter wasn't in any danger. This time.

* * *

For the second time that day Brooke came to an abrupt halt because of the tall dark-haired man. But this time it wasn't to keep from colliding with him, it was because she was stunned. His matching book-ends still flanked him.

Confused, Brooke looked down at the little girl whose hand was firmly tucked into hers. She was a dead ringer for the other two.

Somewhere, Brooke decided, there had to be an overheated cloning machine given over to producing tight, almost jet-black curls, rosebud mouths and big, luminous blue eyes with lashes any grown woman would kill for.

"They're triplets," the man said in answer to the silent question she knew had to be written all over her face.

"I noticed."

She was addressing the top of his head. He'd lowered himself to his knees, wrapping his arms around the tiny recipient, nearly burying her in them.

"Tiffany, where did you go?" he asked.

Tiffany? This was Tiffany? Brooke looked down at the little girl, feeling foolish. She should have known better than to think a grown man would look that worried about a missing wife.

"Into her store," the child said matter-of-factly, pointing a finger at Brooke. "She's got the best books, Daddy. You gotta see them."

"Maybe later," he told her.

Regaining control over emotions that had been, only moments ago, stripped raw, he rose to his feet and looked at the woman beside his daughter. He'd learned to be a quick judge and at the same time not to trust his first impressions. But she looked harmless enough.

Not everyone was a threat, he reminded himself.

"I'm sorry if she caused you any trouble."

Judging by his tone, Brooke thought, Tiffany was probably every bit the handful she appeared. Brooke's eyes swept over the three impish curious faces. Maybe they all were. "No, no trouble at all. As a matter of fact, she was delightful."

If it weren't for the fact that their clothes were slightly different, Brooke wouldn't have been able to tell them apart. Her sympathy went out to the man and his wife. "Are there any more at home like her?"

"No, three's about all I can handle." He laughed softly, the deep sound undulating around the otherwise quiet early-morning mall. "Actually, more than I can handle, as you just saw. I should have grown a third hand the day they were born." There was no mistaking the affection in his voice. He tried to pull his face into a stern expression as he looked down at his prodigal daughter, but failed. "Tiffany, what did I say about wandering off?"

Tiffany drew a deep breath before answering. "Not to."

Out of the corner of his eye, he saw the woman shaking her head and laughing to herself. "What?"

"Nothing." But because she didn't want him to think she was laughing at him, she explained, "It's just that when I heard you calling Tiffany a few minutes ago, I thought you were looking for your wife.''

"No." There was a quiet stillness in his voice. "I wasn't."

Uh-oh, looks like you've just trod on some toes, Brooke upbraided herself. Maybe she'd been hanging around children too long and absorbed their tendency to be too honest, she thought.

If he was about to say anything else, it was put on hold by his two other daughters, both of whom were determined not to remain on the sidelines for a second longer than necessary.

"I'm Bethany," one announced.

"And I'm Stephany," the other told her.

Dutifully Brooke shook first one hand, then the other. "Pleased to meet you, Bethany and Stephany. I'm Brooke."

"And he's Daddy," Bethany nodded behind her at her father.

Brooke raised her eyes to his face. Amused by the introduction, she couldn't help asking, "Does Daddy have a name?"

Was it her imagination, or had he hesitated before putting his hand out? "Tyler Breckinridge," he told her after a beat.

He sounded so formal she wondered if the name was supposed to mean something to her. Was he known for anything? This was Southern California and you were as likely to run into someone famous as not. She'd once eaten dinner one table over from a movie star who'd won her young heart years ago. Out of makeup, it had been hard to recognize him.

She looked at Breckinridge closely, then decided he was merely being formal.

"Brooke Carmichael."

She slipped her hand into his and shook it firmly. She saw a flicker of mild surprise in his eyes. He was probably accustomed to softer women who barely touched hands. Her father had always believed that a firm handshake was the mark of character, and she, he'd told her, had character to spare.

Brooke nodded in the general direction of her bookstore. "I own Tell Me a Story. I found Tiffany taking inventory of my books." She smiled at the little girl. "Please feel free to drop by anytime with the girls." Her smile broadened. "Tiffany can show you the way."

Tiffany needed no more encouragement than that. "How about now, Daddy?"

Two more voices joined in, turning the entreaty into a choruslike refrain. "Yes, please, Daddy?"

"Please, Daddy?"

Tiffany turned up her face toward her father, triumph written all over it. "Three against one, Daddy."

"I already told you, Tiff, this isn't a democracy." He looked at the other two. They had joined ranks with their sister. "It's a dictatorship."

If he meant that to be a no, he was going to have to be clearer than that, Brooke observed. Tiffany had already caught hold of her father's hand and was pulling him toward the store.

"C'mon, Daddy, please?"

Breckinridge never stood a chance, Brooke thought. One look at his face told her that. The girls obviously held him in the palms of their hands. Just as she and Heather had held their father in theirs.

Idly, she couldn't help wondering if the same was true of the girls' mother.

Chapter Two

"Sorry about the bars."

Brooke inserted her key into the lock and the green wrought-iron vines began to climb to the ceiling before they disappeared into the opening, leaving the entrance accessible.

"I'm a little shorthanded this morning, and while I'd like to believe in the goodness of my fellow man, I'd rather not leave temptation standing blatantly in front of him, either."

Remaining where she was, Brooke pocketed the key. She knew enough to stand out of the way. Three could be a formidable number at times.

Like the first fireflies of summer, the three little girls scattered in different directions the moment they entered the store, guided in their selections by the murals that graced the walls. Bethany went to the learning section, Stephany gravitated to the area that abounded with fairies and elves, while Tiffany decided to explore the section that had a bevy of cartoon characters beckoning in welcome.

Watching them, Brooke smiled half to herself, half at the girls' father. "I guess they all have their own personalities, even at this age." She turned to him. "They're what—five?"

"Six," he corrected. "They're small for their age. And as for their personalities—" he laughed soft-

ly to himself, thinking back for a moment, though in general he tried not to do too much of that "—they're distinct, all right. They never mimic one another except when they try to put one over on me." Even then, he was getting pretty good at telling them apart. At first glance they were absolutely identical. But there were small subtle differences. He'd learned to look for them. "I think they were their own persons from the moment they first opened their eyes in the delivery room."

For a few seconds he allowed himself just to enjoy seeing them pore over the different books the store had to offer. They'd gotten their love of books from him. It was one of the things he could give them, besides his unconditional love.

Rousing himself, he turned to look at the woman beside him. He owed her, he thought. A lot. "I want to thank you again for finding Tiffany for me."

She warmed to the sincerity in his voice. "You're

very welcome, but actually I'd say it was more a case of her finding me."

Brooke paused, wondering if she should say anything further, then decided he should know. It was always best for a parent to have some clue about what was going on in his or her child's mind.

"She told me she was looking for a book on how. to find a mommy."

"Oh."

There was something in his voice she couldn't identify. Surprise? Amusement? She couldn't tell, and it was obvious she wasn't about to get any further clues from him. Tyler Breckinridge didn't strike her as exactly the gregarious type.

Nothing wrong with a man who wasn't glad-handing everyone, she thought. Marc had been gregarious, and look where that had led.

Having done her duty, Brooke glanced around. She supposed she could busy herself with the shipment statement until his daughters made their selections, but she found herself wanting to remain right where she was, standing beside the tall, dark handsome stranger.

"Are you from around here?" she asked. He looked at her so sharply that she almost didn't continue. It took her a second to retrieve her train of thought. "The reason I ask is that my bookstore has been open for a while now and I've never seen the girls in here before today."

"No," he replied quietly. "We're not from around here. We just moved to Bedford recently."

And, he thought, he was still trying to get comfortable amid all the new belongings he suddenly found himself with. Some highly paid, overly degreed bureaucrat's notion of what suited him, Tyler supposed. But at least the girls were having fun, burrowing into this new life they found themselves facing. The resilience of youth never ceased to amaze him.

Brooke nodded. She could see why he had chosen to move here. The city's reputation was excellent.

"Can't beat Bedford for schools, weather or safety." She scrutinized him for a moment, trying to see past the almost unsettling planes and angles of his tanned face and the deep-green eyes to the man beneath. "So, where is it that you're from?"

Dark brows drew together as he regarded her warily. "Here and there. Why?"

"No reason." She lifted a shoulder, letting it drop carelessly. "I just thought I detected a New York accent, that's all." Nothing thick or blatant, just a hint of one when he said certain words.

Tyler slipped his hands into his pockets, looking back to the girls. "No, never been to New York."

Was it her imagination or had he lowered his voice just then? There were only his daughters and him in the store. Who was he lowering his voice for?

God, just listen to yourself, Brooke. You never used to be this suspicious. When was she ever going to be rid of that annoying touch of paranoia that seemed to almost constantly hound her thoughts?

"Have you? Been to New York?" Tyler added when she looked at him quizzically.

Boy, have I ever. But she made no effort to explain the wry expression she knew had twisted her lips. "Once. For a while." *Just long enough to have my heart broken.*

He debated saying anything. He, above all, had come to respect privacy and minding his own business. But there was something in her eyes that prompted him to comment, "I take it that it wasn't a pleasurable experience."

Now *there* was an understatement, she thought. But she kept that to herself. Instead, she said only, "It started out that way, but no, not really."

He wanted to say, "Me, too," but that would be admitting he had been in New York, contradicting what he'd just said. He had to keep track of the lies or they would wind up tripping him up.

Lies were like shoots of ivy, their tendrils reaching out, hooking onto things that came in their path. Spreading until you weren't sure just where they had begun or where they were going.

Turning his back to Brooke, he clapped his hands loudly, gaining his daughters' attention. "Well, have you girls made a decision yet?"

None of them wanted to leave. "Just a little longer, Daddy," Bethany pleaded.

"I want these, Daddy." Coming over to him, Stephany produced a pile she had carefully garnered from the shelves.

Eyes as large as saucers, Tiffany quickly grabbed

a handful of books without looking at their titles. Trying to lug her bounty over, Tiffany wound up dropping them on the floor several feet short of her goal. But her spirit wasn't daunted. "If she gets that many, can I have the same, Daddy?"

Coming over to pick up the scattered spoils, Brooke laughed as she made eye contact with Tiffany. "Ah, eager customers. My favorite."

She was surprised to have Tyler join her, quickly gathering the remainder of the fallen collection. He was attempting to look at least a little stern. "Girls, we talked about this."

Closest to his right, Bethany frowned. "We talked about a lot of things, Daddy."

Brooke knew a brewing storm when she smelled it and hurried to quell the waters.

"You know the best thing about my store, girls?" Rising, she deposited Tiffany's fallen goods on the small reading table closest to her. She could put the books back in their places later. "It's not going anywhere." She looked at the three upturned faces in turn. "Which means that if you each just pick one book, you can come back with your daddy some other time and pick another one. And another after that." She smiled warmly at them. "That means you have something to look forward to. And I get to look forward to seeing you all again. How about it? Sound like a deal?"

She already recognized Bethany as the serious one. Standing beside her father, Bethany nodded. "Sounds like a deal," she agreed. "Okay."

Eager not to be left out, Stephany echoed, ''Yeah, okay.''

''Okay.'' Tiffany sighed, glancing over her shoulder at the surrendered cache that had momentarily been hers. She began rifling through the pile. ''I want this one now and this one later and this one…''

Tyler was tempted to physically separate Tiffany from the books, knowing that of the three of them, she was the one who had a penchant for prolonging things. There was somewhere he had to be within the hour, and he had already lost some time.

But instead of giving in to his feelings, he stepped back. ''Make your choices, girls,'' he instructed. ''Put the rest back and meet me at the register.'' Tyler turned from his trio and looked at Brooke. ''Very nicely done.''

This time the lowered voice was perfectly plausible. Absorbing the amused praise, she smiled. ''I've had lots of practice.''

He glanced at her hand. No ring. Still, that didn't mean as much these days as it used to. Neither did wearing one. He still had his because he felt incomplete without it. As incomplete as he felt without Gina.

''Refereeing your own kids?'' he guessed.

Brooke shook her head. It was her greatest regret. Marc had always told her that children would be something they would discuss seriously ''later.'' For them, later never came.

''No, I don't have any. But I get lots of customers.'' Her gaze swept over the girls, who were still solemnly making their choices. "And I've always loved kids. I worked at a preschool when I lived in New York."

Tyler envisioned an arena of screaming children, all vying for attention at once. That had been his one and only experience with preschool. After that, Gina had taught the girls at home, inviting neighborhood children over to make sure that the girls learned how to interact with kids their own age.

"Was that part of the bad experience?" He realized that had to sound as if he was prying. "Sorry, none of my business."

The man was far too polite for a New Yorker. That had to be a different accent she detected in his voice.

"No, it's okay." She waved away his apology. "I don't mind answering. To be honest, that was the only part of the experience that was good. All the way through." She thought of several children who had won her heart and wondered if they still remembered her. "I hated leaving them."

He heard the qualification in her voice and waited. Finally he asked, "But?"

She deliberately pushed thoughts of Marc and his infidelities out of her mind. Why was she suddenly seized with a desire to unburden herself to a perfect stranger? The man had come looking for storybooks, not true confessions.

Brooke tossed her hair, forcing herself to sound cheerful. "But this is home and I needed to come home. You know how it is."

"Yes, I do."

There went her imagination again, reading things into his tone of voice.

But he did sound sad, she thought. Had returning home for him been a bad experience or was it the opposite? Did he long to return home only to know that for one reason or another, he couldn't?

Not her place to ask. It was just going to be one of life's little mysteries, she thought. Like where second socks disappear to between the laundry hamper and the dryer.

The winsome trio interrupted the conversation by trooping up to the register. Each placed her carefully decided-upon final selection on the counter. Tiffany vied for top honors, placing hers on top after Stephany had just done the same. Bethany gave both her sisters the evil eye, meant to quiet them.

Tyler hid his smile. Bethany had always been the one unofficially in charge.

"Okay, Daddy, we're ready," Bethany told him importantly.

"Excellent selections, ladies," Brooke said as she scanned each book in turn, ringing up the sale. The register came up with the final total. She pointed to the figure. "And this, Mr. Breckinridge, is what they all come to."

Stephany looked around, then turned her face up to her father, her small brows drawing together in confusion. "Who's she talking to, Daddy?"

Bethany gave her a reproving look. "That's Daddy's grown-up name," she informed her sister, then looked at her father for confirmation. "Right, Daddy?"

Brooke thought it a rather odd exchange. The girls were so bright about everything else. Why did something as ordinary as formally addressing their father cause any of them confusion?

"Right," Tyler answered. Taking his charge card out of his wallet, he glanced at it before handing it to Brooke.

She could have sworn he looked just the slightest bit apprehensive. Probably wondering if his three little darlings had caused him to max out his card. The man tried to give the appearance of being in charge, but it was evident to anyone who paid the slightest bit of attention that the girls had him tied up in neat little knots around their small fingers.

The authorization number flashed, catching Brooke's eye. She wrote it down on the three-layered credit slip before handing it to Tyler to sign.

He took the pen she offered him and began writing his name. Biting off an oath, he stopped. There was a touch of both frustration and sheepishness in his eyes as he looked up at her.

"I'm sorry, I was preoccupied." His eyes indicated the slip. "I started writing down the name of someone I'm supposed to meet later this afternoon. Would it be too much trouble to write up another slip?"

"No, no trouble at all." She reached into the drawer for a blank slip, then grinned. "I guess being around this handful might make anyone forget their name at times.'' Lowering her eyes, she ran the credit slip through the machine, embossing it, then wrote in the pertinent information. Finished, she held out the slip to him while reaching for the one in his hand.

To her surprise, he ripped it up in front of her, then tucked the pieces into his pocket. ''I'll just get rid of this for you.'' There was no room for discussion or dissent.

Brooke shrugged carelessly. It made no difference to her one way or another. ''Been the victim of credit-card fraud lately?''

He looked up from the slip he was carefully signing. ''What?''

She nodded toward his pocket. ''You're so careful with the receipt I thought that maybe someone had stolen your credit card before. You know, once burned, twice leery, that sort of thing.''

''Yes, something like that.'' Finished, he handed the signed receipt to her, exchanging it for his card. He slipped the latter back into his wallet.

Nothing wrong with being careful, she thought, watching him. She smiled as she handed the large colorful bag with the girls' purchases to him. There was a sleepy-eyed teddy bear, dressed in a nightshirt and nightcap, sitting and reading a storybook with his picture on the cover decorating the side of the bag. Stephany oohed over it.

My father would have been touched, Brooke thought. The teddy bear, Wandering Willie, had been his creation. "He was my favorite, too, when I was your age."

Tiffany's eyes widened. "Is he that old?"

"Tiffany." Tyler flashed Brooke an apologetic look. "Everyone over ten is old to Tiffany."

She'd taken no offense. "I remember how it was." On impulse, Brooke rounded the register and walked them to the entrance. "Well, Mr. Breckinridge, you and the girls feel free to come back any time."

The girls took the invitation as a signal to gang up on him again. Brooke was getting the distinct feeling that they did that a lot. She wondered which side his wife took.

"Can we come back tomorrow, Daddy?"

"Yeah, can we?"

"Please?"

"We'll see," he answered, but he had a hunch it was a foregone conclusion that they would be back, if not tomorrow, then soon. Besides, the woman was genuinely kind to his daughters. That put her store on the plus side. He smiled at her over his shoulder as he ushered the trio out. "Thanks again for all your help."

Brooke inclined her head. "Anytime." She completely missed her sister, entering from the opposite direction, until she almost turned into her.

Unmindful of the near collision, Heather stared at the departing quartet, specifically its tallest member. "Wow. Now there's a man who looks good coming *and* going."

Brooke could only shake her head as she retreated into the store. Heather's official course of study at the university was child psychology, but there were times Brooke was convinced her younger sister's real major was men. She certainly went through her share of them.

"Hello, Heather, so nice of you to finally decide to join me."

Heather deposited her purse behind the counter with the kind of carelessness that came from someone who was carrying nothing worth stealing. "Don't get snippy. My alarm clock didn't go off."

A knowing look creased Brooke's face. "Was that before or after you threw it against the wall?"

Heather pried the lid off the café latte she had bought from the coffee shop. "I only did that once and that was because it woke me up when I had a terrible headache." She sniffed. "I've been very nice to my alarm clocks ever since." She ran her tongue along the inside of the lid before throwing it out, then sidled up beside Brooke. "And never mind me, just how did you help Mr. Gorgeous and just what did you mean by 'Anytime'?"

Leave it to Heather to put the wrong spin on things. "One of his daughters wandered into the store. I helped reunite them, that's all."

"Obviously winning his undying gratitude," Heather commented. She looked at Brooke, her eyes bright. "Sounds like a good beginning to me."

Brooke knew where this conversation was going, and for once, the train was not going to leave the station. "In case you hadn't noticed, little sister, the man has three daughters."

"So?"

"So?" Brooke shut her eyes. There were times Heather was incorrigible. "So that usually means one wife somewhere."

Taking a long swig of her coffee, Heather remained undaunted. "Not necessarily in the present tense." She followed Brooke as she began replacing the books that had been part of Tiffany's original selection. "Maybe he's divorced and he's got custody of the kids."

Brooke turned around to look at Heather. Her sister had gained a thin white mustache, courtesy of the latte. Brooke paused to wipe it away with the tip of her thumb. "And your reasoning for this being?"

"Most dads don't shepherd their kids through a mall in the middle of the week if there's a mommy in the immediate picture," Heather informed her smugly. "They do it on the weekends if they do it at all."

Brooke remained unconvinced. "Maybe he's trying to be nice, give his wife a break." She inserted a tall storybook in between two others, careful not to bruise the spines. "He said they'd just moved here recently. Maybe she's home unpacking and needed some time to herself."

Heather drained her container, then sighed. "Why are you always so willing to look at the gloomy side lately? I can remember when there wasn't a pessimistic thought in your head."

"Yeah, well, so can I, but then I grew up," Brooke said. "And what gloomy picture? There's no gloomy picture. There's no anything. We're just speculating about a customer."

"You're speculating about a customer, and I'm speculating about a possible hunk." Crumpling the container, Heather tossed it into the wastebasket. "I mean, he's a hunk either way, but the question is, is he an available hunk?"

"No, that isn't the question, because that doesn't interest me in the slightest."

Obviously frustrated, Heather threw up her hands. "And that's exactly what I'm worried about. When are you going to get over it, Brooke?"

Brooke had no idea why her temper suddenly snapped. She'd been fine a minute ago. "Over what? Marc?" Her laugh was entirely without mirth. "I was over him the minute I filed for divorce."

Heather shook her head. "I don't mean over him—I mean *over* him."

Brooke stopped replacing books and looked at her younger sister. There was no one she was closer to, but that didn't mean the sisters understood each other all the time. "Are they teaching you English in that college of yours?" She looked back at the last book she was holding, trying to remember where it went. "Because if they are, I'd ask for my tuition money back if I were you."

"You know what I mean." Heather moved

around until she could look directly into her sister's face. Brooke was trying hard to ignore her.

That had never stopped Heather before. "Over what Marc did to you. Just because he cheated—"

Brooke looked at her sister sharply. "Cheated?" she hooted. "Cheated is having a one-night stand, not a touring season. Or seasons, as the case was," she said. "I think the only one Marc didn't wind up getting naked with was the mayor's wife and her dog, and that was probably only because he couldn't arrange a convenient meeting."

Heather knew all about Marc. Her sister had broken down one night and given her all the gory details. Aside from seeing red, her main emotion had been concern about her sister's health, until Brooke had assured her that she'd had herself tested for every sexually transmitted disease possible. She'd done it despite Marc's assurances that he had taken proper precautions. The way she saw it, nothing he said was trustworthy.

Heather continued to press her sister. No matter how awful her ex-brother-in-law had turned out to be, it was time to leave the past behind and move on. "Still, one rotten human being doesn't damn the whole species."

"Maybe not," Brooke allowed, "but it certainly makes you stop and think, doesn't it?" An almost bitter reproachful smile twisted her lips. "About how blind you can be."

Heather slipped her arm around Brooke. Five years younger, she was taller by two inches. "You loved the jerk. You saw what you wanted to see and he was clever.''

Brooke wasn't about to excuse herself. ''I thought I saw what was there.''

Heather wasn't going to stand by and let her sister beat herself up. ''You tended to think the best of everyone, remember?''

''Yes, I remember. But that was the old me. I've grown up.'' Squaring her shoulders, she stepped back. ''I'm a lot more suspicious now.''

Heather looked at her thoughtfully. There was nothing more in this world she wanted than to have the old Brooke back. The one who could laugh without reservation. Love without reservation. ''But not a lot happier, are you.''

Picking up the shipping list, Brooke waved her hand at Heather. ''Practice your child-psychology skills on someone else, little sister.'' She waved the list in front of Heather's face. ''In the meantime, we have a large shipment of books to distribute over the shelves. Let's get to it.''

Heather gave her a smart salute. ''Aye-aye, Captain.''

''Good.'' Brooke nodded. ''Obedience. I like it. And while we're at it, you can tell me exactly why you only got three hours' sleep last night.''

Heather stopped short. ''Four, and how did you know?''

Brooke grinned. ''Because we live in the same house, remember? And I can hear the front door. And even if I couldn't, I know you, little sister.''

She laughed as she threw an arm around Heather affectionately. ''So, tell me all about it.''

That was as close as she intended to get to a date for a long, long time.

Chapter Three

Three leagues beyond bone-tired, Tyler sank into a recliner that was as close in size, shape and color to the one he'd left behind as he could find. It was the one piece of furniture he'd selected himself. The girls were in the family room, finally settling down to enjoy their new books. They'd had lunch in and dinner out, and somewhere in between, he'd done a fair bit of organizing around the house, but not nearly enough.

He looked at the clock in the den, wondering when he should become concerned.

Tyler passed his hand over his eyes, struggling to sort out his feelings from the quagmire he constantly seemed to find himself in. Mentally he took off his hat to Gina.

Until these past nine months, he'd had no idea just how much was involved in raising three children, let alone girl children. Never mind triplets. It was close to mind-boggling.

Gina had been the one to do most of the work, do it so well that he hadn't even been aware that there *was* work involved. She had managed to make raising three girls look effortless. Gina, with her coal-black laughing eyes, had completely fooled him into thinking it was easy being a parent.

It wasn't.

And even love wasn't enough, though it helped smooth over a great many rough spots and blunders he'd made. It was hard doing what was required, what was needed, especially since half of him felt as if it was permanently gone.

He hadn't recovered from being without Gina.

There were times, in the dead of night, when he felt completely overwhelmed by what he faced. When he didn't know if he could actually manage and continue doing what was being asked of him.

But ultimately there was no way around it. He knew he had to do it. And he had to do it alone.

Time, everyone had said, would help him heal. Time was sure taking a hell of a lot of itself about it. The irony made him shake his head.

Impatience burrowed into the weariness, making itself known. He raised his eyes to the clock again.

She was late.

He felt a pang. Maybe Carla wasn't going to call tonight. Maybe she couldn't get away. They'd both agreed that she wouldn't call him from the house. There could be consequences, and it was too much of a risk to take, even though everything so far appeared to be going smoothly.

But appearances could be deceiving, and he wasn't about to take chances. Not with his sister's life and certainly not with the girls'. Losing Gina had been far more than enough for him to endure.

The telephone on the side table next to him rang, slicing through the faraway sound of his daughters' voices. Tyler quickly covered the receiver with his hand and yanked it up to his ear.

"Hello?"

"Is this the party to whom I am speaking?"

Dark half-formed thoughts vanished into the evening. "Very funny, Carla. I thought maybe you weren't calling tonight."

"Things came up." He could hear the unspoken apology in her voice. "I couldn't get away. Enough about me. How's everything with you?"

He looked around the room with its unpacked boxes of possessions that had never been his. Possessions that gave credibility to the life he had assumed. The room reflected his life, as well. "Chaotic, utterly chaotic."

The voice on the other end laughed with distant memory. "Sounds just like you. Are the girls adjusting?"

Pride whispered through him. His daughters were resilient and undefeatable. "Better than me."

"They're younger," she said. "You've got more

to deal with. But you'll get used to it.'' She paused, then added, ''You were always good about rolling with the punches.''

He wished he shared her optimism. Wished it could snake its way through the phone lines and infuse him. Just long enough for him to get beyond the walking wounded and begin to move on. But it'd been nine months, and all he was doing was still going through the motions.

''I'm not now, Carla. This time it feels like I'm down for the count.''

''Not you. Never you,'' she said. ''Look, I'd better go, just in case.''

He glanced at his watch and realized that she must have looked at hers. Wariness had become second nature to him. ''You didn't use the same public phone, did you?''

''I'm not an idiot.''

He laughed, affection sneaking forward. ''The jury's still out on that.''

''Still have that wry sense of humor, I see.'' And then her voice became softer, more serious. ''I miss you.''

He wished she wouldn't say that. But even so, the words comforted him. ''Yeah, me too.''

''Watch your back.''

''Always.'' It was never himself that he was concerned with. He had to be careful for the girls' sake. Until he could be sure that everything was really truly over. Finally over. ''Same time next week.'' It was more of a hope than a question.

"I'll try."

He couldn't ask for any more than that.

Tyler hung up and looked thoughtfully at the telephone. The only thing he had of the past was a disembodied voice whispering in his ear for the briefest of calls. Anything longer might be asking for trouble, at least for now, and trouble was the one thing he had to avoid at all costs.

So far, the cost had been very high.

A small figure stood in the doorway. Tyler separated himself from the past and returned to the present.

"Daddy, you promised to read to us."

He rose. There were now three of them eagerly spilling into the room. "So I did. Which story shall I read first?"

"Mine."

"No, mine."

"Me first, Daddy."

Three books from three different sets of hands were thrust at him from three different directions. Tyler smiled to himself. *Here we go again.*

"Okay, where do you want this, Oma?" Brooke asked. Her father's mother had been "Oma," the German word for grandmother, to her ever since she could remember.

A grunt accompanied Brooke's question. Unable to see, she felt her way into the kitchen, shuffling as she went. But there was good reason for that.

Somewhere on this floor was Jasper, her grandmother's longtime pet. Thirty-one pounds of terri-
torial, caramel-colored, generally unfriendly cat.
There was no way Brooke wanted to take any
chances of stepping on him. Jasper was as unforgiv-
ing as they came.

"Right on the table will be fine, dears," her
grandmother called out.

From the pitch, Brooke guessed that the woman
who had spent more than twelve years raising
Heather and her was not in the room with them now.

"Great. Now all I need to know is where's the
table." Behind her, Brooke heard a loud thud. It was
the sound of Heather depositing the box of books
she had brought in with her on the floor.

"Well, I can tell you that it's not here," Heather
announced, blowing out an exaggerated breath as
she massaged one forearm.

Craning her neck as far as possible, Brooke tried
to peek around the box she was holding. Hers was
larger and heavier than Heather's—she'd insisted on
it. She managed to glimpse the edge of the kitchen
table and hoped there was nothing on it as she made
her way over. Finally finding something to rest the
box on, she eased it onto the flat surface.

"It wouldn't have killed you to help guide me,
you know," she said to Heather.

In response, Heather clasped her hands over her
heart, rolled her eyes heavenward and pretended to
sway. "Oh, yes, it would. The pain, the pain."

"You are, you are," Brooke responded before sucking air into her lungs.

She was going to have to get out more, she told herself. There was no reason to feel so winded, carrying books from the car in her grandmother's driveway to her kitchen.

Of course, the books did weigh a million pounds...

Ada Carmichael came into the kitchen, a welcoming smile on her perfectly round face. She looked at the two girls she considered as much her daughters as her granddaughters, each, in her own way, so like their father. Great affection coursed through Ada's veins as it always did whenever she saw the duo.

She looked from one box to the other before pausing to open the one on the table. "So, these are them?"

"These are them," Brooke confirmed. Crossing to the sink, she poured herself a glass of water and drank half of it before continuing. "Seventy-five copies each of *Willie Wanders off to the Wilderness* and *Willie Wanders Home*. The hardback issues." Her father's creations, they were two of her personal favorites. "So, what's up?" She placed an affectionate hand on her grandmother's shoulder. The older woman barely topped five feet, and Brooke towered over her. "Are you planning to go into business yourself selling Dad's books?"

Ada began taking out the books, placing them on the table in piles of five. "Not into business, exactly."

Brooke studied her. She almost always knew when her grandmother was up to something. With an active mind and a body that refused to recognize its chronological age, there were times the woman was hard to keep up with. "Then what, exactly?"

Having made four piles, Ada looked at her oldest granddaughter proudly. "These are for the scouts."

"Scouts?" Suspicion crept into her voice. She glanced at Heather, who merely shrugged her ignorance and went back to paying homage to the sprawled-out tabby on the floor, scratching him behind the ears. "What kind of scouts?"

"Little ones. I think they call them Brownies. Silly, naming them after something you bake in a pan. Do they still call them Brownies?" Ada asked.

"Yes, Oma, they still call them Brownies." Brooke could remember her grandmother taking on a huge group of girls because Heather wanted to experience being a Brownie and there were no Brownie troops in the vicinity. Ada had started her own. Maybe her grandmother was getting nostalgic. "Did you volunteer to help some troop's den mother out?"

"No." Ada smiled at her matter-of-factly as she continued taking out books and placing them in neat piles of five. "I volunteered to be some troop's den mother. Two troops, actually, but the second one's only temporary, they tell me."

Brooke should have suspected something like this was up, but she'd thought that her grandmother had asked for the books because she'd had a sudden whim to donate her father's books to a local school. "Don't you need a short person of your own before you can do that?"

"Not really." Ada laughed at the quaint notion, moving around to gather books out of the box Heather had left on the floor. "And Elaine Wilcox is pregnant."

Again Brooke looked at Heather, but her sister met her with the same uninformed expression. Big help she was. Just who was Elaine Wilcox? "There's a connection here, right?"

"Of course there is. There's always a connection, dear."

"Okay, then, what is it?" Brooke took the books out of her hands, forcing Ada to stop and look at her in surprise.

"She can't lead her troop anymore. Doctor's orders. Something about a delicate constitution, she said. Sounds suspicious to me." Ada shook her head. "But no one else could take over the troop and they were going to have to disband. Same with Sarah Nelson's troop, but she's just laid up with a sprained ankle. I couldn't refuse them." Ada looked into Brooke's eyes. "You remember what it was like. If you could have seen all those long faces..."

"No," Brooke said patiently, "I don't remember what it was like. It was Heather who was a Brownie, not me."

Bemused, Ada could only shake her head. "Oh, I am sorry, dear. Did you miss not being a Brownie?"

Brooke closed her eyes and exhaled a long breath. The conversation was going around in circles. Nothing new there. "No, not really." Opening her eyes again, she pinned her grandmother with a look. Or tried to. "The point is, when and where did you see these long faces?"

Ada reclaimed her stack of books and continued divvying them up. "Monday. When I was driving home from my aerobics class."

Ordinarily Brooke was very proud of her grandmother. A lot of other women of seventy-five had long since retired from life. Ada Carmichael believed in squeezing out every last drop that life had to offer. But this was squeezing it a bit too much.

"Maybe that aerobics class made you a little light-headed, Oma." Brooke looked at the stacks and envisioned little girls to go with them. Energetic little girls. "This is a lot you're taking on."

Ada's eyes met hers, amusement shining in them. "When has that ever stopped me?"

Brooke surrendered. Oma was what people liked to call an indomitable force of nature. There was no stopping her. "You're right, what was I thinking? It hasn't. But maybe someday it should."

"We'll talk about it then." Finished stacking, Ada shifted her eyes to her other granddaughter. "You're awfully quiet this evening, Heather."

Still stroking the cat and getting infinite pleasure out of it, Heather looked at her sister impishly. She'd been biding her time, waiting for the right moment. It was here. "Brooke met a man."

Brooke saw her grandmother look at her with sharpened interest.

Great, just great.

Leave it to Heather to get things all confused and sic Oma on her. Hoping to stem the tide she knew was coming, Brooke countered quickly with, "I meet men all the time in my store."

Rising to her feet, Heather made a futile attempt to brush off the preponderance of cat hair she'd managed to accumulate in the short amount of time. "But this one made her smile. A genuine smile, Oma."

Brooke gave her sister a withering look. Heather hadn't even been in the store at the time. She'd just walked in a moment after Tyler and his daughters left. "How would you know?"

Undaunted, Heather grinned, lifting her chin. "I've got great distance vision." For safety's sake, she got on her grandmother's other side, out of Brooke's reach.

Blocking Brooke's access to her sister, Ada looked up at her. "Tell me more."

I'll get you for this, Heather, Brooke thought.

She shrugged nonchalantly. "Nothing to tell. He has triplets, one got lost, I helped her find him, he was grateful and they bought books." She aligned the piles on the table with one another. "End of story."

Ada looked genuinely saddened. "Pity. Grateful men are the best kind."

Was everyone missing the obvious here? "He has triplets, Oma."

The fact left the woman unfazed. "Was his wife with him?"

"No, but—"

"Aha." Triumph made its appearance in her eyes. Ada cocked her head again. "Nice-looking? Him, I mean."

"To die for," Heather interjected.

"Aha." Triumph went up another notch.

Fun was fun, but this was really getting out of control. Brooke placed her hand over the closest pile of books. "Stop saying that, Oma, or I'll take back the books."

But the books had been temporarily forgotten. "Did he pay cash?"

"No, a charge card." Brooke's eyes narrowed. Now where was she going with this? "What does that have to do with—"

"You have his name, then. Track him down if you like him," Ada said.

Yup, way out of hand. Why did her grandmother insist on trying to match her up? She knew what she'd gone through with Marc, how badly her heart had been broken. She wasn't about to go on that merry-go-round again, at least not anytime soon.

"Oma, I didn't say anything about liking him."

Ada's sharp green eyes went right through her, saying she knew otherwise. "This is the first conversation we've had about a man who wasn't your father that's lasted more than six seconds." Point driven home, she continued, getting down to the practical. "Now then, there are places on the Internet that can cough up entire histories of people if you know where to look."

Brooke felt as if she was standing in the path of a runaway train, and if she didn't do something right now, she was going to be flattened. In self-defense, she picked up a book and held it out to her grandmother. "Tell me more about this Brownie troop."

Ada waved away the question and ignored the book. "You don't want to hear about them."

When pushed to the wall, Brooke could be every bit as stubborn as her grandmother. And right now she was being pushed. "Oh, yes, I do. Passionately."

Momentarily diverted, Ada smiled. "Wonderful. Then you won't mind if I bring them to the shop tomorrow. First thing in the morning. Only one troop at a time, I promise. It'll be our first field trip."

She'd walked right into that one. Brooke shot Heather a look that clearly threatened her with bodily harm if she dared to be late tomorrow.

There were thirty-eight Brownies in all.

Thirty-eight girls under the age of ten wandering through her store the next morning. For the most part, Brooke had to admit that they were quite well behaved.

Nonetheless, it didn't hurt to keep her fingers crossed while they remained in the store.

Brooke leaned in close to her grandmother. Ada was surveying the scene much the way Queen Victoria might have at a family gathering—except with a great deal more amusement. "It looks like a miniature-Scout jamboree in here," Brooke commented.

Ada nodded her agreement, then looked around. There was no one in the store except the Brownies. "I hope I'm not scaring away your business."

Brooke began to deny the allegation, then thought better of it. "It's for a worthy cause."

"Speaking of business, here comes a customer." Ada nodded to her left at the man entering the store. There were three little girls with him. Identical little girls. "That wouldn't be your man, would it?" Ada asked, smiling.

Though Brooke loved the woman with all her heart, she fought the urge to stuff her into the supply closet—just until Tyler left. "Oma, you have got to stop listening to Heather. If you'll excuse me." She began to walk away to wait on Tyler.

"Never with more pleasure," Ada said. If she could have, she would have given Brooke a push to send her on her way. "Heather was right. He is gorgeous."

Brooke wished her grandmother came with a muzzle.

Tyler was looking around the store as she approached, and from where she was, he looked more than a little taken aback.

"Hi, I didn't expect to see you back so soon."

She shifted her attention to the girls. "Finish your books already, girls?"

"Yes," Stephany told her shyly.

Tiffany, it appeared, couldn't take her eyes off the girls milling around the store, all of whom were glamorously older than she and her sisters and, thus, to be looked up to. "Why are those girls all wearing brown dresses? Do we have to wear brown dresses to be here?"

"You can wear whatever you like." Brooke saw that an explanation was necessary. "They're wearing brown dresses because they're part of a group called Brownies. That's the group you join before you become a Girl Scout."

Bethany digested the information before looking up at her father. "Can we be Brownies, Daddy?"

One step at a time, he thought. "We'll talk."

Brooke had the impression that he didn't think scouting was quite right for his daughters. She was getting the feeling that the man was the overly protective type.

"Is this a bad time?" he asked her.

He looked ready to leave and she found herself not wanting him to. "No, a good time. I like business."

Tyler shook his head. She'd misunderstood. "No, I meant a bad time for us to stop by."

She spread her arms, welcoming them all in. "The more the merrier." And then she leaned back and said to him as if in confidence, "You know, it might not be a bad idea at that."

He hadn't been under the impression that they were discussing anything. "What might not be a bad idea?"

"Letting your girls become Brownies." She knew her grandmother would welcome three new members. Nothing Oma liked better than a houseful of kids. "If they're new in the area, I can't think of a better way for the triplets to make friends."

Her enthusiasm wasn't shared. "They can do that in school."

"True, but—" She took her cue from the look on his face. The look that told her she was trespassing. "Sorry. Didn't mean to tell you how to raise your daughters."

With the apology tendered, he felt like a heel. "And I didn't mean to sound as if I was biting off your head." He knew he was still far too edgy about the situation. He was going to have to work on that. "Actually I stopped by to ask if there was any way I could repay you."

The last thing she wanted was for him to feel indebted to her. "For what? I really didn't do anything."

He wasn't accustomed to selflessness and modesty in the same package. He put his hand on Tiffany's shoulder. If he could, he would have had all three fitted with tracking devices. "You have no idea what you've done."

She pretended to go along with the idea. "Well, in that case, I'll take a big-screen TV and a ticket for a round trip to Hawaii."

He laughed. She had an offbeat sense of humor, but he liked it. "The girls were thinking more along the lines of going to that old-fashioned malt shop in the mall that sells candy."

"The big place with the little tables," Tiffany chimed in.

"Please?" Stephany asked.

"We want you to come," Bethany told her.

She knew the place they were talking about. The one with the decadent chocolate sundae. "I think that might be arranged."

He nodded toward the Brownies. "What about them?"

"Heather can handle them." She indicated her sister in the far end of the store. "Besides, they can't stay here forever. My grandmother just brought them by for a short field trip."

"Your grandmother?" he repeated, puzzled.

Pausing for a second to locate her, Brooke pointed Ada out. "That sprightly-looking woman standing over by *Rolphie the Runaway Rodent*."

"Your murals have names?" he asked.

She laughed and the sound charmed him, reminding him of notes plucked on a harp. "My murals are based on cartoon characters."

"You should know that, Daddy," Tiffany said.

He suppressed an indulgent smile. "I guess my education isn't as complete as I thought."

Chapter Four

Surrounded by the trio, Brooke wasn't sure just which of the girls eagerly asked, "So can you go?"

She glanced toward the rear of the store again. Heather was helping several of the Brownies make selections. Second thoughts nudged forward. "Maybe I'd better check to see if Heather is all right with this."

Leaving them at the front counter, Brooke threaded her way into the back. Oma, mercifully, refrained from following her. But she didn't have to turn around to know there was a pleased smile on her grandmother's face.

"This is your store, Brooke. You don't have to ask if you can go on break." Heather's eyes danced as she took in the man in front and shifted back to her sister's face. "Go, go, before they take back the invitation."

"I'm not asking," Brooke corrected. "I'm just letting you know." But she *had* been asking, she thought. Asking and suddenly hoping that Heather would come up with a reason for her to stay.

Where had this sudden nervous flutter in her stomach come from?

She was being idiotic. It wasn't as if this was a date, or even a meeting over coffee. She was just being polite to a customer, nothing more.

"Don't let your imagination run away with you, Heather," Brooke warned. "The man just wants to say thank-you by taking me to the soda shop."

"Tell him there are other ways to say thank-you than by helping you get your daily chocolate fix," Heather suggested.

Brooke began backing away. She didn't want to keep Tyler and the girls waiting. "This way's just fine with me. Besides…" Brooke silently raised her left hand and pointed to the third finger with her other hand, her meaning clear.

"Was that some kind of code?" he asked her when she joined him.

Tyler's question caught her by surprise. Embarrassed, she struggled for a plausible explanation. The last thing she wanted was to underscore her embarrassment by telling Tyler they were talking about him and his availability.

"Um, I was just, um, reminding her to tie a string around her finger. The malt shop's this way," she said unnecessarily, hoping to change the course of the conversation.

Tyler glanced over his shoulder at the young woman remaining in the store. She waved at him, which he thought was rather odd. He looked at Brooke. Two of the girls had gotten between them. "Isn't it usually the string that's supposed to remind a person of something?"

"Heather's too forgetful to remember to tie one on." That sounded a little lame, even to Brooke.

"Is it hard to work with strings on your fingers?" one of the girls asked.

Looking at the child, Brooke tried to remember which one she was. "Sometimes, which is why she forgets to put them on. We're here," Brooke announced, relieved, pausing by the large menu that was mounted on a stand in the middle of the entrance. "See anything you like?"

"Everything!" the girls cried in unison.

She laughed, looking over her shoulder at Tyler. "Girls after my own heart."

He nodded. "Mine, too." His hand lightly pressed against the backs of two of them, he gently herded his daughters inside.

There were no tables for five, only for two and four, so he pulled a couple of tables together. To Brooke's surprise, he helped her with her chair, ushering her in.

"You're very courtly," she observed. "Not that common these days."

He raised his eyebrows. "Offended?"

"Pleased," she countered.

"Me, too, Daddy. Do me."

"Me."

"No, me."

He sighed, pretending to be weary, but the uplifted corners of his mouth gave him away as he did the honors on all three chairs one at a time. "I should have been an octopus."

The girls giggled, except for Stephany, who shivered and closed her eyes.

They were a nice family, Brooke thought. She waited until he sat down himself before commenting on what he'd said when they'd walked in. "You don't strike me as a man with a sweet tooth."

He found himself smiling at the observation. A pervading fondness for chocolate was something else he shared with the girls, as well as with his sister. "Why?"

"Are your teeth really sweet, Daddy?" Tiffany looked at him curiously.

"Shh." Bethany waved her hand at her sister to be quiet.

"It's an expression people use when someone has a weakness for candy," Brooke explained before looking at Tyler. "I just thought it was unusual because you look so…" She searched for a word and settled on "fit."

The smile turned a handsome man into a man who was almost devastating. She found that it took her a second to remember to exhale and then reverse the process.

"Thanks." He looked down at the paper menus on the tables, small replicas of the one at the entrance. "So, what'll everyone have?"

The girls had already made their choices and vied with one another to be first in their declarations. Chocolate, strawberry and vanilla sundaes with pleas for plenty of chocolate syrup were ordered. Brooke wondered if their selection of flavors was a way to tell them apart.

Tyler's dark blue eyes isolated the moment for her, fixed as they were on her face. "What would you like?"

Completely improbable, inappropriate answers popped up in her head. Heather's influence, she thought, dismissing them all.

She found it harder to dismiss the feeling they created. Or the one generated by the way he looked at her.

He probably wasn't even aware of it. "A strawberry-ice-cream soda. This is one of the few places that makes them the old-fashioned way," she told him.

"One strawberry-ice-cream soda coming up," he said, rising from the table and going to the counter to place the order.

"You like strawberry," the triplet sitting directly opposite her observed, beaming. Something told Brooke she had just bonded with the little girl. She only wished she knew which one it was.

"It's the first flavor I ever remember having." She'd been about three at the time. It had come in the form of an ice-cream cone and she had worn it more than eaten it, according to the way her father used to tell the story. She just remembered liking the taste.

Looking over to the counter, Brooke saw that their order was almost filled. Tyler was glancing around for a tray to carry everything back to their table.

"Excuse me," she murmured to the girls. "I think your dad needs help." She made her way over to him. "They don't have trays, don't ask me why. Here, why don't I take three of them and you take the other two?" She anticipated his protest. "I worked my way through college as a waitress," she said. "There's a trick to this."

"You're full of surprises," he commented.

She laughed. "I try. Here you go, girls." She placed the proper sundae in front of the right triplet. Raising her eyes, she caught Tyler looking at her. There was amusement and approval in his eyes. And something more she couldn't quite place.

"Now you've gotta help her with her chair again, Daddy," the strawberry-sundae triplet declared.

"That's all right," Brooke said. "We don't want your daddy's banana split to melt."

As she sat down, she watched all three girls plunge into their desserts with gusto. Pulling the wrapper off her straw, she slipped it into her soda and took a long sip, savoring the taste. Her eyes had drifted closed. When she opened them again, she saw Tyler looking at her.

"I like to enjoy things," she explained, feeling a little self-conscious. She grabbed the first topic she could think of. "So, how long did you say you've been in Bedford?"

The reply came after a beat, gauged in caution. "Not long, really." He had to get over holding everything suspect, he told himself. The woman seemed harmless enough, if someone that attractive could be thought of as harmless. She was only making conversation. Conversation that he, after all, had invited her to make by asking her here in the first place. "Less than two weeks," he added. His look took in the girls who appeared oblivious to anything but what they were eating. But he knew better. "Everything's still very new to us."

"That'll go quick enough. We Bedfordites are a friendly lot," Brooke testified. She paused as she took another long swallow. "You picked a great place to settle. Can't beat the schools here."

"I know. I'm about to become part of that," he said. Relocating to Bedford hadn't been by his own choice, but it had been a good one nonetheless.

"Oh, really?" She looked at him with interest. "What do you teach?"

He thought of the three subjects he'd taken on. "Music composition. Music theory. Piano."

"He used to play the guitar, too," Tiffany volunteered, then lowered her voice to add, "But he gave it away."

Brooke had always loved guitar music. Her father had played the instrument, in addition to the piano, and they'd all sat around and sung, mostly off-key. It didn't matter. "Oh? Why?"

Tyler shrugged, uncomfortable with the question, with the memory. "It demanded too much of my time."

He hadn't touched the guitar in nine months. He'd taken it up for Gina. She'd loved listening to him play. It had pleased him because it was something he could do just for her, without the crowds wanting a piece of him. But there were too many painful memories locked up with playing the guitar to keep the instrument around now. He'd given it to Carla.

Brooke was trying to sort out the information coming in dribs and drabs. "Are you a professional musician on the side?"

He stiffened slightly. Did she recognize him? No, he'd never played out here. But she'd said she'd lived in New York...

He brazened it out. "No, why?"

She shrugged carelessly. "I just thought that was an unusual way to put it, that's all. I've always thought of the guitar as something recreational. A way of releasing tension as you caressed strings and searched for elusive chords that summed up the way you were feeling." That was how her father had put it. It was he who had instilled the love of music in her and her sister. "I never thought of it putting demands on a person."

"I find the piano more satisfying." There were years he hadn't. Years when he'd thought of the piano as something that shackled him. An albatross to drag with him from place to place. A child prodigy, he'd been forced by his father to tour and play and practice, practice, practice. Meeting Gina had set him free.

"It is beautiful," she agreed. Something else he had in common with her father, she thought. "So where are you going to be teaching?"

He'd gone to see the campus yesterday afternoon, showing it to the girls. They'd enjoyed running up and down the wide open spaces nestled between the buildings. Open space was something new to them. Such a change from the penthouse apartment in New York. "UC Bedford."

"Really?" Brooke laughed, shaking her head. "Small world."

He took a drink from his water glass. Tyler saw Tiffany eyeing his all-but-untouched dish and nodded, pushing it toward her and her sisters. "Three ways," he instructed, then returned his attention to Brooke. "Why? Was that the college you attended?"

"No, I went to school back East. But Heather's currently going to UC Bedford. Heather's my younger sister," she added, not remembering whether or not she'd made that clear earlier. "She helps me out at the store between quarters and when she's not swamped with classes."

He'd noticed a faint resemblance. "What is your sister majoring in?"

Brooke finished the last of the soda and pushed the glass away. "Child psych."

Bethany's eyes grew huge. "Does she tell children's fortunes?"

Tyler and Brooke exchanged glances. She had the distinct feeling they were sharing what Heather would have called "a moment."

Brooke bit back a laugh at the little girl's question. "No, honey, she's not a psychic. Psych is short for psychology. Heather wants to help children with their problems." She saw interest bloom in the three small faces. "Not everyone is as lucky as you are to have a daddy who cares so much about you."

Tiffany nodded solemnly, then sighed. "We had a mommy who cared about us, too. But she's not here anymore."

"Tiffany."

The warning was immediate. A contrite expression slipped over the little girl's face, creating instant guilt within Tyler's heart. But he had talked to them about this, told the girls that personal matters were not to be trotted out in front of strangers. Especially not this personal matter. They didn't quite understand why, but they knew when not to bend the rules, and this was one of those times.

He silently placed a hand over Tiffany's. The sadness vanished from her eyes.

His wife was dead, Brooke realized. That would explain why he was still wearing the ring and why he had three little ducklings following in his wake. Brooke began to fill in the blank spaces. Her eyes met his. "I'm very sorry."

Tyler saw her looking at his wedding ring. Alive

or not, there was still a bond between him and Gina. "So am I. I didn't mean to sound so abrupt just now." Debating for a moment, he knew that silence would only seem odd. He told her as much as he could. "My wife died nine months ago, and I'm afraid I haven't gotten around to taking this off yet."

So, they still made princes once in a while, she mused. Just her luck to have married a frog. "I find that incredibly romantic. I didn't think there were men like you around." She could see by his expression that he was puzzled. Not wanting to go into any aspect of the marriage she'd just as soon forget, Brooke gave him a cursory answer. "Loving, faithful. You've given the girls a wonderful foundation. My father was like you."

It was what had blinded her to Marc's faults, she supposed. In her naiveté she'd thought all men were created equal.

"Oh?" He bent to pick up the napkin Stephany dropped. "He was a musician?"

Confused, she looked at him. Hadn't he just denied being a musician?

She couched her question politely. "I thought you said you were a teacher."

He handed the napkin back to Stephany. "A man can be both."

He sounded a little guarded, but then, she supposed, so was she, despite her open manner. Maybe he didn't like admitting to having been a musician. Depending on the type, some not-so-flattering notions were associated with the life of a musician.

"True. My father was an illustrator for children's books. Eventually he began writing the stories, as well as illustrating them." Pride came into her voice, as it always did when she talked about her father. "He did the Wandering Willie series, as well as Rolphie and a few others."

Tyler made the connection. "Then he was the one who painted your murals?"

She only wished he had. It was because of the money he left her that she could manage to open a bookstore, but she would have given it all up in a heartbeat just to have him back for a day.

"No, I did that. My father passed away a little more than two years ago."

She'd flown home to take care of him when Heather had told her he'd become too ill to work. She'd taken a hiatus from her teaching position, preparing to stay for however long her father needed her, but there had been no need for elaborate preparations. The end came abruptly, robbing her of the few months the doctor's prognosis had tenuously promised her.

Arriving back in New York early had been a real education for her. She'd found Marc in bed with a nubile lab technician. It heralded the beginning of the end of her marriage. The two blows, one coming on the heels of the other, had left her reeling.

"But he passed on his love of art and children to both my sister and me—in varying degrees. I paint better than she does, but she's a better musician."

Music had always interested Tyler, even in the

years he'd tried to break away. "What do you play?"

She grinned. "A little guitar, a little piano. Very little piano."

Restless, Tiffany was ready to pop up like toast from her seat. "We've got a piano in our house. A big one. You wanna come see?"

Tyler didn't look pleased about the impromptu invitation, Brooke noted. She couldn't help wondering how many strangers the girls invited over. "Maybe someday."

With the invitation on the table, the moment felt awkward. Finding a safe route, Tyler reinforced the invitation in the vaguest of terms. "You're welcome to visit once we're settled in."

Brooke caught on immediately. She'd become a master of the vague statement herself. The invitation had been given conditionally. Tendered, but safe, since there was no date attached to it. Just as well. She had no intentions of starting something with this man even if he did have a gentle sexy charm about him.

"Thank you, I'll keep that in mind."

"Today?" Stephany added her small voice to the conversation. "It's unpacked."

"It's almost the only thing that is," Tiffany added.

Brooke shook her head. "I'm afraid I can't today. I've used all the free time I can spare today by having this decadent ice cream."

Puzzled, Bethany's small brows drew together

and she looked at her father. "What does deck-a-dent mean, Daddy?"

Brooke thought she heard him murmur, "Something you won't have to deal with for a long time."

She searched for an answer the girls could understand. "It means something that tempts you to do something you shouldn't." She indicated the banana split the girls had all but finished off. "Like this ice cream. It could tempt anyone to give up their diet because it looks so good and tastes even better."

Stephany was still wrestling with trying to understand. "Then deck-a-dent's a good thing?"

Bethany frowned. "Tempting is never a good thing," she said matter-of-factly, then stole a look at her father for confirmation.

Brooke backed up. "Well, not everything tempting is bad. When you smell something good baking in the oven, that's tempting..." She could see she wasn't making it any clearer. "Okay, this is more complicated than I thought." Brooke flashed a sheepish smile at Tyler. "I do have several children's dictionaries at the shop that might help. They're a lot better at explaining words than I am."

Fierce in her loyalties, Tiffany jumped in to defend the woman she had taken such a liking to. "I think you're very good at explaining things. I understand." She looked at her sisters, waiting to be challenged.

Brooke didn't bother trying to suppress her laughter. She looked at Tyler over their heads. "Have I told you that your daughters are delightful?"

Tyler greatly preferred hearing praise for the girls to having his own work commended. "My problem is that they know it, and they use it to try to get away with a lot."

Whatever they got away with, Brooke had a feeling he didn't really mind.

"Do you have kids of your own?" Bethany suddenly wanted to know.

This time, the look Tyler gave his daughter was sterner. They really did know better. What had come over them today? "We don't ask people personal questions like that, Bethany."

The girl's crestfallen look was too much for Brooke. "That's not really personal. It's not like you asked me what size dress I wear, right, Bethany? No, I don't have any kids of my own. But I'd like to someday."

Stephany looked at her timidly. "Does your husband like kids?"

"I don't have a husband." It felt good to say that. The very thought was ironic, because there had been a time when she'd wanted nothing more than to be Marc's wife.

Bethany looked at her thoughtfully. Brooke could almost see the wheels turning in her head. "Don't you need one for kids?"

Out of the mouths of babes. Brooke tried to look properly serious. "Absolutely right. I guess I'm going to have to put that on my shopping list."

Tiffany covered her mouth with her hands. "You can't shop for a husband."

"Oh, really?" Brooke leaned over the table, one girl to another—completely winning all the girls over with this single gesture. "Well, how would *you* find one?"

Tiffany didn't even have to think about that one. "I'd ask Daddy where to find one."

Tyler found the exchange between Brooke and his daughters amusing. "I want you to remember that answer fifteen years from now," he told Tiffany. "I'm going to hold you to it when you bring home some scruffy character for me to meet."

Her father hadn't wanted her to marry Marc, Brooke remembered, but she'd thought it was because he didn't want her moving to New York permanently. Looking back, she realized he'd probably seen something in Marc that love had blinded her to. She wished she'd paid more attention then.

Tyler noted the look on her face and saw discomfort. "I'm sorry. The girls shouldn't be prying."

"Oh, no, that's all right. I'm enjoying this, really." She smiled at the girls. "This has been one of the nicest breaks I've had in a very long time." She looked at the remainder of the banana split. The girls had all had their share, but there was still some left. She hated seeing things go to waste, especially delicious things, but she wouldn't have been able to fit in a single bite more. "Too bad I can't take this with me in a doggie bag."

"You have a doggie?" There was longing in Tiffany's voice.

"It's a 'spression, silly," Bethany told her haughtily, remembering what Brooke had said before. "You don't have to have a doggie to have a doggie bag."

Amused, Brooke looked at Tyler. "I take it Bethany is your scholar."

His eyes touched his daughter's face with a pride Brooke could easily recall from her own past. "I think the others call it being a know-it-all."

Nothing unusual there. "That's what sisters say to each other."

Stephany cocked her head. "Did you say that to your sister?"

"No," Brooke said honestly, "but she said that to me. A lot. I'm older."

Hungry for friends, Stephany was jockeying for her own position of favor with this new person in their lives. "You don't look older."

"And this one is your diplomat," Brooke declared to Tyler.

He ran his hand over the girl's dark silken hair. "A rather shy diplomat."

She was beginning to be able to tell them apart. "That would make Tiffany the fearless one," Brooke concluded.

"I like you. You say nice things." Tiffany looked at her father. "Can we take her home with us, Daddy? Please?"

He knew where that was coming from. They

missed a woman's presence. As did he. But there was no replacing what they had lost.

Brooke felt a little like a stray puppy. Time for the puppy to come to Daddy's rescue, she decided.

"Tell you what." Three faces looked at her expectantly. "I'll come visit as soon as your dad says he's ready for visitors. But right now, I'm going to say thank you for the very lovely reward and go back to rescue Heather."

Her choice of words brought about another round of questions. "Is she in trouble?" Tiffany asked.

"Can we help?" Bethany wanted to know.

"Was that another 'spression?"

Brooke took on the questions one at a time. "No, she's not in any real trouble, but thank you for offering to help and yes, that was another expression, but possibly just a little closer to the truth than expressions in general." Leaning over, she surprised Tyler by extending her hand to him. "Mr. Breckinridge, it's been a pleasure. Enjoy your girls. My dad used to say that they grow up much too fast."

She heard one of the girls, Stephany she assumed, whisper shyly, "I like her, Daddy."

Brooke regretted that she was too far away to hear his reply to that.

Chapter Five

"So, how did it go?"

Brooke rolled her eyes. She might have known that Heather would be lying in wait for her. "You know, you could wait to pounce on me until after I walked into the store."

Leaning over the main counter, Heather pointed to the floor. "Technically, one step over the line places you inside the store," she said triumphantly. "It's like when the tires of a car are over the crosswalk when the traffic light's still yellow."

Brooke picked up her name tag from behind the register and pinned it on again. "My, my, ever since you've been dating that policeman, you've just become a walking wealth of information."

Heather paused to straighten Brooke's slightly

askew name tag. "It's not going to work, you know."

Forcing a smile to her lips, Brooke nodded at a woman who'd just walked in with her little boy. "Good afternoon." She lowered her voice. "What's not going to work?" she asked her sister.

"You're not going to divert me with talk about Simon." Heather had been going out with the rookie cop since May. It was casual, but it was fun. Something she was convinced her older sister needed in her life right now. "I want to know how it went with Mr. Luscious." Momentarily forgetting that there was a customer in the store, she looked at Brooke, her eyes shining with hopeful enthusiasm. "Was I right? Is he available in the true sense of the word?"

Brooke thought of Tyler's expression when he'd spoken about his late wife. "In the true sense of the word, no." Suddenly she realized that the store was almost deathly quiet. Brooke looked around. "Where's Oma and the brown horde?"

"Gone," Heather said impatiently. "She promised them a visit to Toyland next."

Brooke shook her head. Where did the woman get that kind of energy? She knew people half Ada's age who paled in comparison. "God bless you, Oma. That woman takes more on herself than any three people—"

Heather's impatience piqued. "Yes, yes, we both think Oma's wonderful. That wasn't up for debate." She leaned in closer so that the woman in their store wouldn't overhear. "What do you mean, not in the true sense of the word? Is he still married?"

"No, his wife died, from what I could gather." In an effort to get away from Heather's interrogation, Brooke picked up the Halloween decorations she'd brought in with her this morning. Halloween was almost two months away, but she knew first-hand that anything to do with it attracted the younger children, and she'd always believed in prolonging festivities for as long as possible.

Doggedly, Heather followed her as she began hanging up genial-looking ghosts and friendly witches. "Then what's the problem?"

Brooke paused. The front legs of the black cat she was holding came loose, instantly turning into long thin black accordions. "The problem is that he seems to have enough on his plate with the girls, relocation and starting at UCB."

To forestall a lecture, Heather picked up another decoration as if to mount it on the wall. Instead, she held on to it as she talked. "He's a student?"

Brooke looked around for the right place to hang the cat. "No, a teacher, silly." Dragging over a footstool, she stood on it and attached the cat to a ceiling fixture. Air began to move the crepe legs. The little boy in the store, watching intently, giggled.

Perfect, Brooke thought, getting down.

"A teacher of…?" Heather waited for a response. None came. Brooke looked utterly absorbed in finding the proper place to hang the next decoration. "I swear, Brooke, getting information out of you is like pulling teeth. Worse." Regret filled her eyes as a touch of nostalgia pushed forward. "Where's the babbling Brooke I grew up with?"

Brooke had too much work to do to get embroiled in this kind of conversation. "Hadn't you heard? There's been a drought."

Heather sighed, shaking her head. She'd been waiting for Brooke to bounce back for a long time now. "You know, if you let Marc get to you like this, he's won."

"Won what?" Pushing the stool back against the wall, Brooke saw that the woman who'd entered earlier was standing by the register with her son. "I'll be right there," she called to them, then lowered her voice. "It wasn't a contest," she told Heather. "It was supposed to be a marriage."

"It was life." Heather followed her to the register. "Sometimes you get dealt a rough hand. But you don't just drop out of the game."

Temporarily ignoring her sister, Brooke was all smiles for the little boy standing by his mother. She read the title out loud as she rang up the sale. "*Wendell Steals Home*. Great book. You're going to love it." She leaned over to the boy. "My dad used to read this one to me when I was your age."

Clearly shy, the little boy smiled up at her as his mother paid for the purchase. Once they were gone, Brooke turned back to Heather, the thread of their conversation far from forgotten. "And I'm not dropping out of the game."

Heather shook her head, unconvinced but secretly hopeful. "Could have fooled me."

Being honest, Brooke had to admit that she was no longer the carefree outgoing woman she'd been before her disillusionment and divorce. "I'm just being more cautious before I bet the farm again."

A glimmer came into Heather's eyes. "Seems to me that the barnyard animals should be getting restless right about now."

Brooke's eyes narrowed. She looked around to make sure no one else had entered the store. "Heather."

Heather kept one eye on the entrance. Since there were no small ears to hear, she was going to have this conversation with her sister. She only had Brooke's best interests at heart. "How long has it been since you've been with a man?"

Brooke crossed back to the box of decorations and began taking them out one by one, placing them on the counter. She avoided looking Heather in the eye. "I just went out for a soda."

Leaning closer to Brooke's ear, Heather said emphatically, "In the biblical sense, my dear."

Brooke dearly loved her sister, shared almost everything with her, but there were times when Heather could be a real pain in the behind.

"That's private," she snapped.

Heather sighed. "Yeah, that's what I thought." Temporarily retreating, she gave her sister space.

Guilt rode up on a black charger almost instantly. She hadn't meant to snap at Heather like that. She gave the silence between them less than two minutes. "He's a music teacher."

Turning from the display she was straightening in the aftermath of the Brownie invasion, Heather looked at her, not sure if she'd imagined Brooke's voice. "What?"

Brooke surrendered. She couldn't stand the idea of having hurt Heather's feelings, justifiably or not. "You asked me before what he teaches. The triplets' father," she added. "He's a music teacher." Heather stopped straightening and crossed back to her. "I get the feeling he's a professional musician, too, or was. One of the girls said something about playing the piano."

Heather's eyes crinkled. "Maybe you could audit one of his classes, then the two of you could, oh, I don't know, tickle each other's ivories some evening."

Heather was incorrigible. Brooke turned on her heel, leaving the decorations for the time being. What she needed was a little legitimate peace and quiet. "I've got inventory papers to find."

That was one way to put it, Heather thought. "Better start moving that stock before no one wants it," she called after Brooke.

Brooke stopped just short of the back-room door. "You know, with all these metaphors flying around, maybe you're wasting your time getting a degree as a child psychologist. Maybe you should go out for an English major. Unless, of course, they give degrees for being a royal pain at that university of yours.''

Heather pretended to think. ''Not at present, but I might slip it into their suggestion box sometime.'' Picking up a decoration, Heather looked around for somewhere to hang it. ''What did you say his last name was?'' she called to the back room.

Brooke stuck her head out. ''I didn't. It's Breck-inridge. Why?'' In response, she heard Heather laugh to herself.

''I thought so.''

Curious, Brooke came out of her office. ''Thought what?''

''Gretchen said there was this really hunky new teacher in the Studio Arts Department.'' Her eyes were fairly dancing. ''Better put your claim on him before a lot of would-be music majors beat you to it.''

''Customer.'' With relief, Brooke pointed toward the store entrance. ''And if anyone wants me, I'll be in the back room.''

Heather watched her go. ''Coward.''

Coward.

Alone in the store this morning while Heather ran personal errands, Brooke frowned to herself. Heather had said the word teasingly the other day, but it had haunted her ever since, mocked her. She was beginning to wonder uncomfortably if maybe there wasn't at least a germ of truth in the label.

Brooke had never thought of herself as a coward.

On the contrary, she'd always rushed out and grabbed life with both hands, no matter what. Her mother's death had devastated her at a young age, but it hadn't destroyed her. She'd always felt it was her obligation to meet life head-on, even when she wasn't feeling very brave. Because she was the older one and Heather looked up to her.

And because her father was trying so hard to raise them. She never wanted to give him any more trouble than he already had. Ever since she could remember, she'd tried to be a buffer, for both her father and her sister. Somehow she'd mistakenly thought that had made her tough. Impervious to pain.

It took Marc to make her realize that she was wrong. That in this one sensitive area, where her heart was concerned, she was as vulnerable as a person could possibly be.

Her mistake, she supposed, reflecting now, was that she'd believed wholeheartedly in the integrity of others. She'd been raised that way by a father who'd taken life's blows on the chin and continued not only to remain standing on his own two feet, but to see only the good in every situation.

Bringing a slew of Halloween books to the front of the store, Brooke piled them on the counter before putting them in the proper dumps for display.

She supposed that in a way, she was dishonoring her father's memory by letting a jerk like Marc blot out her father's lessons.

Even now, after two years, it was hard to move

beyond the hurt and resentment. She'd been such a
fool. On the surface Marc had been everything she'd
always wanted. Bright, funny, intelligent, not to
mention exceptionally handsome, he'd come from a
solid scandal-free well-to-do family. She'd fallen in
love on first sight. She'd fallen for him while he'd
merely been falling for her species.

When she'd met him, he was studying to become
a doctor. She hadn't realized at the time that he'd
been studying to follow his life's fantasy: playing
doctor. When she finally caught on to what was happening, her world had come crashing in on her like
a house of cards.

Heather was right. One rotten apple didn't spoil
the barrel. However, it did spoil Brooke's appetite
for apples. She couldn't see herself venturing out
into the orchard any time soon. And certainly not
with the naive enthusiasm she'd once felt.

One by one, she began placing the newly gathered
books on the display. Though she wouldn't tell
Heather, and despite her resolve, her thoughts kept
returning to the handsome music teacher and his
brood. There was just something about him...

What had he said the other day in reply to his
daughter's assertion that she liked her? Brooke knew
he'd commented on what Tiffany had said because
she distinctly remembered hearing the low murmur
of his voice. Had she gotten a thumbs-up or a
thumbs-down?

Or had he simply said, "Finish the banana split,"
to his daughter?

No sense in wondering, she told herself. She wiggled in a tall thin book between two of the same height but greater width. Unless Heather got it into her head to bag the man on campus and drag him to her doorstep—something she was going to adamantly warn her sister not to attempt under penalty of death—there was little to no chance she'd ever see the man again.

"Hi."

Looking up, Brooke dropped the book she was holding. Tyler was beside her in a flash, picking it up and handing it to her. She didn't bother looking at what she was doing as she pushed the book onto a shelf. Her eyes were riveted to him.

He was here.

Trying to seem nonchalant, she dusted off her hands on the back of her jeans.

"Hi, where's your entourage?" She nodded at the conspicuously empty space behind him.

"They're in school," he replied.

The mass return to school for grades twelve and under had gotten under way yesterday. She'd forgotten about that, since Heather's classes didn't begin until the end of the month.

"So, what brings you here? Looking for a little back-to-school present for the girls?" Oma had always gotten something for her and Heather when they had mournfully watched the end of summer approach. Looking forward to a "surprise" had made going back to school that first day not quite as dreadful as it might have been.

The girls managed to wangle gifts out of him on a fairly regular basis. That wasn't why he was here. Tyler felt a little awkward about asking. He didn't know the woman that well. But he knew her better than he knew anyone else in Bedford at the moment and she might be in a position to know.

"Actually what I'm looking for is help. You wouldn't happen to know of someone who's looking for a job, would you? I'm going to be teaching at the university soon, and I need someone to pick up the girls from school each day and stay with them until I come home."

Tyler looked so uncomfortable all she could think of was putting him at ease. "You're looking for a baby-sitter?"

He shook his head. Damn, he hoped she didn't think he was hitting on her. The thought had just occurred to him. Maybe because it also occurred to him that they were standing alone in the store and for some reason, she looked more attractive to him than she had the previous two times he'd seen her.

"More like a part-time nanny. Just to fill in the hours I'm not there." He needed to explain why he was here and not at some agency that handled these sorts of positions. He wanted a recommendation someone wasn't getting paid to render, and he'd really liked the way she'd interacted with his girls.

"I wouldn't ask, except that I really don't know anyone around here yet, and I thought that since you deal with children, you might know someone who's qualified." Looking into her eyes, he noticed for the first time how hypnotically blue they were. He felt himself floundering. "They've got agencies for this, but I thought a recommendation coming from someone like you might be more genuine... Maybe this wasn't such a good idea, after all..."

The man looked as if he was going to turn on his heel and bolt any second. Without thinking, Brooke caught his arm.

"No, wait, it's not a bad idea at all." Realizing she was holding on to him, Brooke let go.

Oma was at loose ends. There was no other explanation for why she'd taken on the Brownie troop in addition to everything else she did. Anyone could see that Oma clearly missed being around children.

"Do you remember the woman who was here the last time you and the girls came to the store? The day you and the girls took me out for a soda?"

Tyler remembered the day very well. At least her part in it. "You mean your sister?"

Heather wouldn't have been a bad choice, either, if this was summer. But if it was summer, he wouldn't have needed anyone. "No, the other woman." She saw that he was coming up blank. She continued with the description. "Short, full-figured woman with a wreath of grayish hair—kind of looks like Mrs. Claus in search of the elves. She had Brownies with her."

The image vaguely registered. "Oh, yes, right. Your grandmother," he recalled.

The fact that he remembered pleased her. "Well, what about her?" Brooke asked.

He wasn't sure he was following Brooke. What he was becoming aware of, however, was that her smile had a way of penetrating a man and going straight to his core. It made him want to smile as well. But that wasn't why he was here. "What about her what?"

She'd thought her question was obvious. "As your nanny. I'm sure she would be more than happy to take on the position. I can vouch firsthand that she's absolutely wonderful with kids. She's never met one she didn't like. And vice versa."

It was tempting, hearing such an unconditional recommendation. But Brooke's grandmother was a little older than he'd had in mind. He thought of his trio and hesitated.

"I don't know. No offense, but she seemed a little…" There was no way to put this tactfully, and he didn't want to insult Brooke or her family. "Well, she'd need a lot of energy to keep up with Tiffany."

Brooke laughed. The man was in for a surprise. Oma could probably tire him out. "Not to worry. She could keep up with the Tasmanian devil if the occasion arose. When we were kids, Heather and I had trouble keeping up with her, not the other way around. She's very vital and active."

Still, he had his doubts. He'd had an interim nanny for them while he'd waited for the trial to unfold, and the woman had quit after three weeks, too exhausted to continue. "I'm sure, but…"

Obviously the man needed a little convincing.

Brooke began listing a litany of some of Oma's activities. "Besides the Brownies, she volunteers at the local hospital one to two days a week—she reads to patients and brings around the juice cart—and does volunteer dog walking at the animal shelter another couple of days. We've always had trouble getting her to sit still for a family portrait. She's accustomed to being on the go."

Tyler felt himself being won over. By both the potential nanny and her granddaughter. "So it would seem." A touch of amusement played along his lips. "Won't this interfere with all her volunteering?"

Brooke laughed. "You don't know my grandmother. She's the type who likes to squeeze in as much as she can into a day. Simply put, the more she has to do, the more she does, no ifs, ands or buts. Or excuses."

Brooke's eyes shone radiantly as she talked about her grandmother. It captivated him even though he didn't want it to. "I guess energy runs in your family."

Without realizing it, Brooke cocked her head the way her grandmother did. "Excuse me?"

Amusement grew into almost a grin. "You're talking almost faster than I can listen."

It wasn't the first time she'd been accused of talking too fast. The shrug was marginally self-conscious. "Sorry, I do that when I get excited. I know Oma's been dying to take on more than she's been doing lately. That's why she agreed to lead the Brownie troop."

"Oma?" Was that the woman's first name? Tyler wondered.

She'd been using the term her entire life and at times forgot that not everyone knew what it was. "It means grandmother in German."

"Are you? German, I mean?" Tyler asked.

"One-eighth or something like that." There was such a mixture in her background that she considered herself an all-American mutt for the most part. "Oma's grandmother came from Germany. Oma told us she'd always liked the sound of the word, so when Heather and I came along, she taught us to call her that. Said it sounded a lot nicer than Granny." A fond smile lifted the corners of her mouth. "She thought being called 'Granny' made her feel old."

"From what you just told me, I don't think anything can make her feel old."

Brooke looked at him, realizing that she was standing perhaps a little closer than she should be. But to step back would be conspicuous. So she remained where she was, trying to keep her mind on the topic and not on the fact that the cologne or aftershave he was wearing was mildly arousing. As was the man. "So you'll see her? For the job?"

He thought of the orientation sessions the department chairman was holding for incoming students. That was just around the corner. Tyler had preparations to make if he was going to pull this off, and fast. "She'd have to start on Monday."

Brooke grinned. "No problem. A little juggling

of responsibilities and she could probably start to-morrow afternoon.''

"Think a lot of her, don't you." He found such family loyalty appealing.

Thinking a lot of Oma didn't begin to cover it. She and Heather adored the ground Oma walked on. "There's nobody in the world like her." Looking around, she found a paper and pencil. "Now, if you'll just give me your phone number and ad-dress…"

He hated the way suspicion automatically leapt into his throat. But there it was, full-blown and thick, choking him. "Why?"

Brooke looked at him. She could have sworn she heard wariness in his voice. Again. Why? Nothing remotely suspicious was being said. "So she can call you for an appointment and come over for an interview."

Idiot, he upbraided himself. Hoping she hadn't noticed, Tyler took the pencil and paper from her and began writing. "Sorry, I'm just not used to giving it out."

He wasn't the first man to guard his privacy, she supposed. But as a parent, he was in for a rude awakening. "Wait until the girls bring home their annual enrollment packets from school. It'll feel like everyone but the local grocery store is going to have your address and phone number."

Maybe it was her imagination again, but he looked disturbed by the joke she'd just made.

Chapter Six

Ada Carmichael set down the large tin of chocolate chips she'd just dipped into and scattered them into the fresh batter. She directed an amused interested look at her granddaughter. "Are we talking about that to-die-for guy with the triplets who was in your store the day I brought the Brownies in?"

Rather than call, Brooke had decided to let Heather handle the last few hours at the bookstore and dropped by her grandmother's house to discuss Tyler's need for a nanny. This wasn't the sort of thing you casually broached over the telephone.

Her mouth full of cookie, Brooke nearly choked. "To-die-for? Oma, where do you get this stuff?"

Ada gave her a look her late husband was fond of describing as mysterious. "I don't 'get' it from anywhere. It's always been there, Brooke." Showering in bits of walnuts, she mixed the batter one last time. "Just because my birth certificate qualifies me for senior-citizen discounts at the movies doesn't mean I'm dead." She leveled a sharp look at Brooke. "I crochet shawls because I like to, not because that's my only interest in life." Her smile broadened and she continued mixing. "Nothing like a good-looking man to make you appreciate the finer things in life." Her eyes were positively sparkling as she began dropping spoonfuls of cookie dough onto the greased baking sheet.

"I'm not sure I should bring the two of you together," Brooke said.

Ada dusted off her hands. Slipping one hand into an oven mitt, she picked up the tray and slid it onto a rung in the oven. "That's okay, honey, I won't touch him. He's all yours."

"Oma, come on. The man is new in the area and doesn't know anyone else. He just came to ask me if I knew anyone who might be interested in filling the position. He wanted a personal recommendation, that's all."

Turning from the stove, Ada smiled knowingly. "Just that position?"

Brooke rolled her eyes. "My God, Oma, I'm going to have to start monitoring the kinds of people you hang out with."

The timer went off. Bending, Ada took out a cookie sheet from the bottom rung of the oven and placed it on a hot plate on the table. "Maybe you'd better start monitoring the kind *you're* hanging out with. Or not hanging out with,'' she added significantly. ''I'm beginning to worry about you, Brooke. You sound older than Howard's mother.'' Howard was one of the men Oma had been seeing lately.

Sighing, Brooke picked up another cookie and began eating it, slowly breaking off soft bits. Oma had a far more active love life than she had, but Brooke was okay with that. She wanted the tranquillity that came with not putting yourself out there to be hurt.

''Oma, I came to ask you if you'd be interested in working as the girls' nanny, not to hear another lecture about how I shouldn't be sitting on the sidelines of life. I get enough of that sort of thing from Heather.''

Ada spared her a short penetrating look over her shoulder. ''Obviously you haven't gotten enough of that sort of thing from Heather, otherwise it would have stuck by now.'' She turned around. ''And when have I ever lectured you? I make suggestions, which you are free to take or not take.''

As if that was true for one minute. ''And free to listen to why I'm wrong if I don't do what you suggest.''

Still, Brooke couldn't fault her. Oma only did it because she cared. Oma and Heather both cared. She just wished they'd care a little less vocally.

Ada pointed at her with the tip of her spatula. ''Exactly. I'm glad we understand each other.'' She smiled, thinking of the three girls and the proposition. It had been a while since she'd had a hand in raising children. She missed the satisfaction that came from nurturing. "And I'd love to help out the young professor. When does he want me to begin?"

There she went, at a full gallop again, Brooke thought fondly. "First, I think he'd like to go through the formality of an interview, Oma." A smile tugged at her lips. "It might make him feel a little more, um, secure."

"Secure?" Oma cocked her head, confused. "Secure about what? Do I look like Ma Barker?"

Brooke rolled her eyes. Another one of her grandmother's fascinations was with the earlier half of the 1900s and women who made their mark on the right and wrong side of the law. Ada Carmichael had been into equality between the sexes decades before it had become popular.

"He probably doesn't even know who Ma Barker is, Oma. I don't think Tyler Breckinridge's into gangland thugs and their molls."

The thought left Ada unfazed. "Well, then, I'll just have to teach him." She flashed a grin comprised of perfect teeth. "And Ma Barker was no one's moll. She led the gang." Satisfied that enough time had lapsed, she began removing cookies from the tray and gingerly placing them on a plate. "So what's he like, this professor? Casual or formal?"

Brooke considered before answering. If first impressions were correct, the man didn't have a casual bone in his body. "Actually I'd have to go with formal. At least, he seems that way to me."

Ada nodded thoughtfully. "So, you'll have to loosen him up."

Oma had to stop this, Brooke thought. What if her grandmother started dropping hints around Tyler? She'd never be able to look him in the eye again—provided the opportunity even presented itself again. "I have no intention of loosening the man up or doing anything else with him, for that matter."

"Pity." Cleaning off the cookie sheet, Ada sprayed the surface with cooking oil and began dropping more dough on it. "I think you both might benefit from a little interaction." She paused, hand on one hip as she scrutinized her granddaughter. "How long has it been since you interacted with a man, Brooke?"

She'd sat still for enough interrogation for one evening, Brooke thought. She hopped off the stool. "That's it, I've done my good deed. I'm going." She paused to take an extra chocolate-chip cookie. She figured she'd earned it. "You're just too young for me, Oma."

"And you, my darling, are too old for me." Brushing her hands off on her apron, Ada took Brooke's chin in her hand, her eyes serious. "You've all the time in the world to be old, Brooke. It happens much faster than you think. Be young as long as you can. Please."

A smile curved her mouth as her grandmother released her chin. "Like you?"

Ada shrugged carelessly, though she was pleased. "You could do worse."

"I know." Brooke kissed her cheek. "Thanks, Oma."

"For what?"

"For the cookies." She held up the one in her hand. "For saying yes." Her eyes touched the other woman's face with love. "For being you."

"You remember to do the same." Ada turned back to her baking. The neighborhood school was holding a bake sale the next day, and she meant to contribute. "Let me know when he wants to interview me."

"Will do."

But first, Brooke thought as she left, she was going to have to find that out herself.

It might have been simpler to make a phone call. Just pressing seven little numbers on her keypad, that was all. But this was good news and Brooke wanted to see Tyler's reaction.

She supposed, after all that talk with her grandmother, she just wanted to see him, if only to prove to herself that she really wasn't affected by him. After all, the man was good-looking, but the sun didn't rise and set around him.

So, instead of going home, Brooke found herself driving by the development where Tyler lived with his daughters.

Slowing her car at the foot of his winding street, Brooke chewed thoughtfully on her lower lip. Tyler had looked uneasy about giving her the address to begin with. How was he going to react to seeing her on his doorstep?

Happy, she decided, once she told him why she was there.

Her life with Marc had her seeing shadows where none were and being suspicious of perfectly normal reactions. Tyler had looked a little uncertain earlier only because he didn't know her that well, and you don't give out your phone number and address to every Tom, Dick or Harry that comes along. Or Brooke.

Nothing strange about that.

Oma and Heather were right. She was going to have to stop this kind of skepticism if she hoped to maintain her sanity. Or to ever have a sane relationship with anyone, never mind a romantic one.

Approaching the house whose numbers matched the ones on the paper in her hand, she heard the sound of a piano concerto drifting out the open windows.

The soothing music quickly surrounded her, melting through her skin, its long misty fingers slowly drawing away the tension that had been traveling with her, making it a thing of the past.

He was good, she thought. Very good. Her father would have been impressed.

Jonathan Carmichael had always wanted to be a professional musician. But with two young daughters to raise, he had to be practical. So he'd given up the notion of a musical career, sacrificing his dreams for Heather and her.

She never forgot that.

Brooke tightened her hands on the steering wheel. For a moment she considered just driving away rather than interrupting Tyler. But she knew he'd been anxious about finding someone to stay with the girls. He'd want to hear about this as soon as possible. And then there was the interview to arrange.

She had no idea why she felt nervous approaching the door.

She rang the doorbell three times before the music stopped.

She heard the sound of footsteps crossing tile, growing louder. But rather than unlocking the door, the peephole was opened first. After a moment it silently closed again, and then she heard a chain being removed and two locks being flipped. If this had been the 1920s, she would have said she was being inspected in order to gain entrance to a speakeasy. Maybe she should have knocked three times and asked for Joe, she thought, amused.

The door finally opened.

Glancing at the hardware on the door, she nodded a greeting at Tyler. "You sure you're not a transplanted New Yorker? Back there, we all triple-locked our doors."

He indicated the back of the door. In addition to the regular lock, there was a dead bolt. "Just two locks."

"And a chain," she said. He was still standing there, blocking any entrance. Maybe that was his subtle way of telling her to go away. She asked, anyway. "May I come in?"

"Sorry." He stepped back, allowing her entrance. "I should have realized that you didn't stop by to count how many locks I have on my door."

Walking inside, Brooke saw that there were large unopened boxes scattered throughout the immediate area, some in the hall, others apparently stilled in their march into the living room. It looked as if he couldn't make up his mind whether he wanted to stay or go. The furniture he'd uncrated all appeared to be new.

Must be nice, she thought, to have all new things like that.

Getting her mind back on why she was here, she turned to look at him. "I came to ask you when you'd like to see my grandmother."

He looked at her blankly. "Your grandmother?" And then he remembered. Seeing her on his doorstep had completely thrown him off. "Oh, right, for the job."

He seemed preoccupied. Had to be the music. She remembered that when her father immersed himself in playing, it was as if he was in another world.

"I drove over to Oma's house and asked her if she was interested." Now that she thought about it, it seemed almost a silly question, given whom she was asking. "She's eager to get started. You'll find that out about her. There isn't anything Oma does by half measures. I guarantee that your girls will be in wonderful hands if you hire her."

He thought for a moment, trying not to get distracted by the way the light coming through the skylight shimmered on her skin, bathing it in different brilliant hues. She looked almost ethereal. ''I've got some free time tomorrow. Would ten o'clock be all right for her?''

Oma had made it sound as if she would be flexible. ''It'll be perfect.'' He'd hung a few paintings on the wall. Expensive paintings, judging by the frames. So much for the idea of a poor struggling music professor. She noticed the pensive look on his face. He was the picture of a concerned father. ''Don't worry, you'll love her.''

That was asking a bit much, he thought. He'd never connected easily, except to his music. Until Gina. She had taught him a different way, but that light had gone out of him.

''I don't need to love her. I just need to know that she's responsible and can handle emergencies.''

The use of the word *emergencies* didn't surprise Brooke. Becoming a parent suddenly made *emergencies* a part of everyday vocabulary.

''Not to worry, Oma's Red Cross certified in first aid and CPR.''

To be both sounded a little like overkill to him. ''Was she a nurse at one time?''

''Oma was a little bit of everything at one time,'' Brooke informed him fondly. He looked unconvinced. ''Some of her friends are older than she is, and she likes being prepared.''

He thought it a good trait.

"Brooke!"

Hearing her name uttered like a joyous war cry, Brooke looked up to see one of the triplets at the head of the stairs. The next moment the little girl came sailing down, the other two following in her wake.

Brooke was waiting at the bottom, arms wide open. "It's like watching a commercial for a photocopier come to life," she said over her shoulder to Tyler, laughing as the first triplet launched herself into her arms.

Tiffany, she decided. This had to be Tiffany. She had the mark of ringleader about her.

"What are you doing here, Brooke?" Bethany wanted to know, losing no time in claiming a piece of her.

Stephany said nothing, but she smiled broadly as she nestled against Brooke.

She was completely surrounded and she loved it. "Telling your dad about the lady who'll be watching you while he's working."

Tiffany stepped back, dropping her hands. A defensiveness came into her eyes. "We don't need anyone watching us. We're old enough to watch ourselves."

"We are," Bethany agreed. "And we don't need anyone like Miss Houston."

Turning, Brooke looked at Tyler. "Miss Houston?" Had he already interviewed someone for the position?

Tiffany answered before her father got the chance. "Yeah, she was our nanny when we lived in—"

"That's enough, Tiffany," Tyler cut in sharply. And then, because they couldn't begin to understand the danger in talking about who they were and where they came from, his voice softened. "Don't bore Ms. Carmichael with details she doesn't want to hear."

Brooke had the definite impression that he'd caught himself before saying *need* rather than *want*. Just what was it he was afraid the little girl would blurt out? Was he some kind of criminal? She found the idea of a criminal on the lam with three little girls in tow fanciful, to say the least.

Tiffany looked properly chastised for a few seconds before her sunny smile returned, brighter than before. She grabbed Brooke's hand, commandeering her attention.

"Did you hear our daddy play the piano?" She gave her father a fawning look that was guaranteed to make him feel guilty. "Doesn't he play pretty?"

"I certainly did and he certainly does." Brooke looked at Tyler and smiled. "Made me almost want to run to a piano and finger a few keys out of nostalgia."

Tiffany had absolutely no idea what *nostalgia* meant, but she could solve Brooke's longing easily enough. "We've got one right here in the living room. Wanna play it?"

The look on Tyler's face was not exactly inviting, although in truth, she had to admit it looked rather amused more than anything else. Again, she got the feeling that he gave in a great deal to his pint-size trio.

Still, she did attempt to demur. But she suddenly found each hand caught up by a triplet, with the third leading the way past towers of boxes into the living room.

"I really don't think I should," Brooke finally managed to say. "Not after hearing the way your daddy played."

Tyler found her sudden reluctance strangely appealing. He hadn't thought of her as being shy. Following in the girls' wake, he joined Brooke at the piano. "Why?"

"The difference between the way you play and I play would be something akin to the difference between 'The Moonlight Sonata' and 'Chopsticks.' I just know the basics and not much beyond that. Besides, it's been a while since I played." She hadn't touched the keyboard since her father died. There had been no reason to. It was him she had always played for.

Tyler saw what he took to be a hint of longing in her eyes. There had been a time when he had turned his back on the piano himself. But music was something that got into your blood, like a passion, and never really let go. "Please, go ahead. I didn't mean to make you feel self-conscious."

Too late.

The little girls looked at Brooke eagerly, though she had absolutely no idea why it seemed to mean so much to them to have her play. Brooke ran her tongue over her lips, debating.

"I don't generally like making a fool of myself…" Maybe it was her imagination, but she could have sworn the girls drew closer, tightening the ring around her as if that could somehow forge a magic circle, infusing her with the power to do anything she wanted. Brooke relented. "But seeing as how it's for a good cause, okay." She sat down at the piano and haltingly began to pick out a song she had committed to memory a long time ago. "Greensleeves." One of her father's favorites. "I'm more than a little rusty," she warned.

Tyler didn't seem to hear the disclaimer. Instead, he was watching her hands, she realized. Probably taking her fingering apart to hell.

Forcing herself to continue until she reached the end, Brooke finally lifted her hands from the keys. The sound of small hands clapping warmed her heart, even though she knew the applause was entirely undeserved.

"You play pretty," Stephany told her shyly, using the exact same phrase Tiffany had when she was describing her father's performance.

Brooke caught the small chin in her hand, pressing a kiss to the girl's forehead. "And you lie sweetly."

Not to be left out, the other two quickly pushed their way in, both exclaiming that they thoroughly enjoyed the song she had played.

"It was one of my father's favorite songs," she

told them. She felt her eyes misting. Terrific. The man was really going to think she was strange, tearing up over "Greensleeves." Trying to cover for herself, she raised her eyes to his face. "Remember, you asked for it."

He shook his head at the excuse. "You don't play as badly as you think."

She supposed that was a compliment. "I couldn't possibly."

To her surprise he sat down beside her. "What you lack isn't technique, exactly."

Did he realize that his leg had brushed hers when he sat down? An unexpected salvo of heat shot up her limb, sending out tributaries as it went. She found her voice. "Then what, exactly?"

His eyes held hers. "Confidence."

"Yes," she agreed, "there's that. But it might have something to do with the fact that when I drove up to your house, I heard music coming out that could have made angels weep."

Tiffany's face scrooched up. "Daddy can make angels cry?"

"But I liked it," Stephany protested.

Only Bethany looked at Brooke knowingly. "Another 'spression, Brooke?"

Brooke smiled broadly, unable to resist giving the girl a hug. "Another expression," she agreed.

"And only an expression," Tyler interjected. When she looked at him, skepticism in her eyes, he told her, "You could play like that, you know."

Brooke laughed. The man was kinder than she'd

thought. "In your dreams." She looked at the keyboard, running her fingers over it. "I only learned to play the piano because it meant so much to my father."

Tyler thought of his own father. Stereotypically tyrannical, the man had demanded hours of practice from him once he'd reluctantly and enviously acknowledged the talent that Tyler had been born with. Tyler never got over the feeling that his father couldn't forgive him for being better at something than he was. Trotting him out to perform like a trained monkey had been his way of getting even.

"Why? Did he play professionally? Or was he trying to live his dreams through you?"

She found the second question rather odd. "Neither, but he would have liked to have played professionally. Piano, guitar, drums—he played them all." If she closed her eyes, she could still see him, spending hours searching for the right note, the right chord, looking for elusive melodies, which eventually came to him. "Loved them all."

He assumed her father would have pursued his love. The way his father had attempted to pursue his, until he'd discovered he wasn't good enough to garner the attention he craved. "So why didn't he?"

"Because he was selfless," she volunteered before Tyler finished his question. "He loved us more. Heather and me. And he felt we needed a parent who was at home. There was Oma, but he felt she wasn't enough. That he owed it to us to be around. So he gave up his dream. For us."

Tyler tried to reconcile that with what she'd told him earlier. "I thought you said he wrote and illustrated children's books."

"He did." Her father was one of the most gifted people she knew, and she felt lucky to have had him in her life. "And he did love it, but not the same way he loved music. There was always something playing at our house." She laughed, looking at the girls who were incredibly quiet, listening to her. "Half the time it was him."

"What you need," Tyler said out of the blue, "is someone to teach you proper fingering."

"You can do it, Daddy," Tiffany said.

"Maybe I can," he agreed after a moment.

Brooke had no idea why something small and distant within her felt as if it was suddenly contracting.

Chapter Seven

Feeling just the slightest bit flustered, Brooke ran her tongue over her dry lips. She wasn't quite sure what he was telling her, but she was reasonably certain he hadn't just offered to give her piano lessons. The man had made it clear he was too busy.

"Does that mean I get a performance, up close and personal?"

Tiffany immediately took up the battle cry. "Play something for her, Daddy," she pleaded, fairly jumping up and down.

"Yes, play something for me, Daddy," Brooke echoed, fixing a grin on her lips while silently ordering her stomach to settle down, for heaven's sake. It wasn't as if the man was propositioning her.

But when Tyler looked at her like that, languidly

taking measure of her, Brooke felt a fresh major flutter of nerves.

Telling herself that it was an utterly adolescent reaction didn't have the desired effect. The fluttering continued.

When his other two daughters chimed in, Tyler gave in. "All right."

Taking a seat beside Brooke on the bench, he played the same song she had so movingly that it brought tears to her eyes, not just because of the memories it stirred, but because this time the notes, so deep, so rich, seemed to go right into her soul. Drawing emotions out while cocooning her with a gentle warmth she hadn't realized she needed until it was there.

His playing left her almost breathless. And momentarily speechless.

She flushed, embarrassed by the way she'd just played the same song. "Now I *really* feel like burying my head in my hands."

Because his intentions had been so completely different, her response confused him for a moment. And then he understood. "I didn't do it to show you up. I played the same song to show you what it could sound like, given time."

"Time, right. I figure about a hundred years should do it, give or take a quarter of a century," Brooke quipped. There were very few times she was completely out of her depth, but this was one of them. "Not to mention an influx of talent."

He'd decided a long time ago that modesty, like

egotism, was generally a waste of time when it came to music. "You have talent," he told her matter-of-factly. "The first major step in playing well is wanting to play well."

That sounded like something printed on a T-shirt from a specialty store. She begged to differ with him. "Desire is not always the answer."

The sentence seemed to melt away from her lips as their eyes met.

"No," he agreed quietly, "it's not." And right now, for some inexplicable reason, desire was exactly what he was feeling. Shaking it off, he continued, "But it's definitely a major step in the right direction."

Was it her, or did it suddenly get ten degrees warmer in the room? Trying hard not to appear obvious, Brooke let out a long breath.

It didn't help.

"Here, let me show you," Tyler offered, focusing back on the music and not the way her lips parted. He arched his hands over the proper keys. "Place your fingers on the keys like so."

Brooke did her best to mimic what she saw. "Like this?"

He shook his head. "Not quite." When Tyler rose from the bench, she assumed he'd given up and the lesson was over. But the next thing she knew, he was behind her, leaning over so that his face was next to hers as he placed his hands over hers. "More like this."

She was trying very hard to pay attention, she

really was. But between her self-consciousness and the flash of uninvited heat, the contact of skin to skin made it hard for her to concentrate. She could feel the warmth of his body against her back, could feel his breath on her cheek as he lowered his head to look at her hands.

Brooke was everlastingly grateful that a racing heart wasn't loud enough to be heard by the human ear.

Tyler felt her pulse quickening beneath his fingers as he slipped them down her hands, over her wrists. He interpreted it the only way he could. She was feeling awkward.

He turned his face into hers. "I'm sorry, am I making you nervous?"

Even as he asked, he discovered that his poise was deserting him, ever so slightly. Being this close to her was having a peculiar effect on him.

"No!" She realized that had come out a bit too emphatically. Backtracking, she offered him a quick smile as the girls looked at her curiously. "Yes. I mean, I do better alone."

"Some people do." The way he tacitly agreed gave her the feeling that Tyler was talking about himself, but not necessarily about playing the piano. Brooke could feel her own curiosity growing.

Because the girls were looking at her as if they were waiting for her to continue, she said, "It's just that I like to iron out my own mistakes and then let someone else witness the results." She shrugged, looking at the keyboard. "Such as they are."

He could see she was struggling not to seem uncomfortable. "I didn't mean to make you feel self-conscious."

She didn't want him blaming himself, especially in front of his adoring daughters. Besides, it didn't have so much to do with her lack of expertise as it did with the close proximity of his body.

"It's not you," she lied. "It's me."

He thought of himself and the teacher he'd been fortunate enough to have come into his life. It was more for him than his father that he had finally agreed to go on tour. The decision had had serious repercussions. After years of near exhaustion, he had finally put a stop to the acclaimed nomadic existence he lived.

"It's easier to learn with a teacher showing the way," he assured her.

She glanced at the girls who had become unusually quiet as they listened to the exchange. She could only guess what they were thinking. If she demurred, they might be disappointed in her. The thought bothered her.

She sought another way out. "You're absolutely right, but you've got better things to do than to try to teach me the correct fingering for 'Greensleeves.'"

"Not really." He could see that his answer took her by surprise. The notion was oddly pleasing. "My only alternative at the moment is unpacking. Teaching you a few performance fundamentals seems like a good way to procrastinate."

"Well, since you put it that way..." Brooke raised her hands, bending them at the wrist and wiggling her fingers. "Let the lessons begin."

She was rewarded with giggling from the girls and a smile from Tyler. She felt herself both captivated and motivated.

Maybe, Brooke thought forty minutes later, still sitting beside Tyler on the piano bench, Heather and Oma were not completely off track with their broad hints and blatant suggestions about her getting back into the social swing of things. It would be worth a try—if the man she was trying with was someone like Tyler Breckinridge.

Displaying a soothing patience, he seemed nonetheless determined to get her to at least play this one song in a manner similar to his own.

After several tries Tyler leaned back and studied her. She was trying too hard. Self-consciousness was holding her back. "Again. But this time, get out of your own way, Brooke. Nobody's going to grade you. This is just for your own pleasure, no one else's." He sat forward and gestured toward the keyboard.

All right, maybe she could have fun with it at that. "Okay, cover your ears."

He leaned back again. "Don't think about me. I'm not even here."

Easier said than done, she thought.

"Yes, you are, Daddy. You're right there," Tiffany said, pointing to him.

Touché, Brooke thought, grinning.

She faced the keyboard. It was a matter of honor. She'd be damned if she gave up before she got this just the way he wanted. She might not be able to play anything else the way he'd shown her, but she was determined to get this one piece right.

Closing her eyes, she concentrated. And began to play. When she was finished, she ventured a look in his direction and saw the approval in his eyes.

Why that meant so much to her she couldn't put into words, but it did. She felt an exhilarating sense of accomplishment.

Then, very slowly, he began to clap. "There, how did that feel?"

Euphoric, Brooke looked down at her hands. The credit was his, not hers. All she was doing was mimicking. "As if I was playing with someone else's fingers."

Tyler took one of her hands in his and held it up as if to examine it. "No, they seem to still be attached to you. You did it on your own." He was pleased it had gone so well, and his eyes met hers. "There's nothing in music you can't do if you want to."

He wasn't sure just when it happened, when he realized he wasn't just holding someone's hand, but her hand. Brooke's. And that it mattered.

The moment he did, he spread his fingers and released her. "Well, that was a very good first lesson."

Caught by surprise, she stared at him. "There'll be others?"

He hadn't gone into this thinking of becoming her teacher, but the idea was not without its appeal. He'd enjoyed a sense of satisfaction, watching her find her way to the chords. "If you like."

The girls, apparently feeling that they had been patient long enough, converged around them.

"Now play something together," Bethany suggested.

"Just please not 'Greensleeves,'" Tiffany begged.

Brooke laughed. Her eyes found Tyler's, offering him a silent question. He nodded. Well, if he was game, why shouldn't she be?

She paused, thinking. "There aren't many songs I know straight through. How are you with 'Oh, Susannah'?"

"Ah, the classics." Swinging around again, he made himself comfortable on the bench beside her. "Ready?"

"As I'll ever be."

In the next moment they were both playing the first song her father had ever taught her, she offering a much less complicated rendition than Tyler. By the time they finished, she was laughing. After a beat Tyler joined in. A feeling of warmth surged through her.

Tiffany, in a competition of her own with her sisters, clapped harder. "More!"

But instead, Brooke rose from the bench. "My

father always taught me to quit while I was ahead.'' She smiled her thanks at Tyler. ''I'm afraid I've long overstayed my welcome.''

Tyler got to his feet, as well. ''Did I do anything to make you think that?''

It took very little imagination for her to envision him as a professor. There'd be no nonsense in his class. ''No, but...you've been very kind.'' And she knew she had to be invading his privacy just by being here.

''Not difficult under the circumstances.'' The comment sounded offhand, but she took it as a compliment, anyway.

Getting in Brooke's way, Bethany turned toward her father for a ruling on what she already assumed was a foregone conclusion. ''Daddy, can Brooke stay for dinner?''

''Please, Daddy, we never have anyone stay anymore,'' Tiffany chimed in.

Even Stephany gave him a soulful look.

He was undecided about the wisdom of encouraging the situation—from all their perspectives. But he didn't want to seem rude, either. He left it up to Brooke, hoping she'd take her cue. ''We're just having pizza.''

Did he want her to stay? She couldn't tell. Brooke felt her way across the tightrope, watching his face as she answered. ''Sounds good to me—it'll go well with the chocolate-chip cookies I had as an appetizer at my grandmother's. If I won't be intruding,'' she tacked on.

He'd extended the invitation. He could hardly re-
nege now. Besides, he had to admit that having an
adult to talk to did have its appeal. ''We've played
'Oh, Susannah' together. That makes you practically
family.''

She rather liked the way he put that.

Brooke stayed another hour. They ate pizza off
paper plates. Dishes, Bethany told her, were packed
away somewhere in the myriad boxes, as were the
rest of the glasses.

''They're all new,'' Tiffany added.

Brooke saw the warning look that went from father to daughter and wondered why the childish
words of pride evoked that kind of reaction from
Tyler. There was something here she wasn't getting,
she thought.

Maybe he felt Tiffany was bragging and was trying to nip the trait in the bud before it became a
problem.

Brooke eyed the boxes that populated the rooms
like tall silent brown sentries. ''I could help you
unpack. I'm good at organizing, and it's the least I
can do in exchange for the lesson and dinner.''

''Not necessary,'' he said flatly.

If there had been room for argument, she might
have attempted it, but his tone cut her dead, vapor-
izing the offer. Maybe he had things he didn't want
people pawing through. She could respect that.

He was getting jumpy again, Tyler thought. Not
everyone had an ulterior motive. There'd been no

need to sound so stern. He attempted to mitigate it. "But thanks for the offer."

Brooke inclined her head. The man certainly was a puzzle. "Anytime. Well, I'd better be going."

She said goodbye to the girls, who remained in the house while Tyler walked her to her car. Because he'd apologized, Brooke decided to venture a little further again.

"You might think better of my offer to help after you're surrounded with a million things to put away. I'll leave it standing. Just give me a call if you change your mind." She paused, debating with herself. She didn't want to seem pushy, but she had a feeling that Tyler might need someone to talk to. "I don't usually do this, but since you're new in town and you might have other questions..." She looked in her purse for her business card and a pencil. Finding both, she wrote her home phone number on the back of the card and handed it to him. "That's my number. If you or the girls need something, call me. If I'm not home, the answering machine is." She smiled. "It doesn't get to go out much anymore."

"I can empathize." He looked at her, slipping the card into his pocket.

She felt for the car door, opening it. "Well, thanks again for the pizza and..."

The look in his eyes had her voice trickling away from her, leaving things unspoken.

Moonlight, coupled with longing and loneliness, did strange things to people. He'd always believed that. Had even composed two songs about it, though the words had remained locked in his mind rather than committed to paper. The moon was the loneliest of the heavenly bodies. He could feel its pull right now. Could feel, too, the pull of the woman standing before him.

For the past nine months, he'd lived every day with an emptiness he hadn't known what to do with. Tonight, for a small space of time, he'd forgotten about that emptiness. Forgotten because Brooke's words had somehow filled it. Her words, her laughter.

Her.

Had he thought it through, he wouldn't have done it. But he wasn't thinking. He was reacting. To stimuli from without and within.

As if hypnotized, Tyler lowered his head and touched his lips to hers, kissing Brooke very, very slowly.

For the first time in nine months, he didn't feel as if he was marking time in hell.

He felt alive.

Brooke didn't have time to be startled or even surprised. That would come later. All there was time for now was a deep-seated feeling of pleasure. It poured over her and kept her within its grasp all the while their lips were joined.

The intensity of the kiss kept growing until it was almost all-consuming. She couldn't say with any certainty if it was he or she who'd caused this. Her mind had taken off on a holiday, recording nothing.

She didn't remember threading her arms around

his neck, didn't remember rising on her toes to draw closer to the kiss. Didn't even remember leaning her body into his.

Yet there she was, with all three feats accomplished. And there she was, wanting more.

It had been years since he had kissed any woman but Gina. When she had come into his life, every other woman has ceased to be. Throughout their marriage, he hadn't even been mildly tempted by anyone else.

There was something about this woman that tempted him. Something that aroused him and reminded him, after all this time, that he was still a man with a man's needs.

He was very much alive.

And not happy about it. Because to be alive meant complications. And invited pain.

Her eyes were closed, Brooke realized. When she finally opened them, a second before their lips parted, she saw them. Three little faces, completely identical from this vantage point, gathered at the window. Watching. And smiling.

At least they were happy about this, she thought. That made three out of five, because she didn't know how she felt about this new turn of events, and she suspected the same was true for Tyler.

Maybe this was what they called chemistry. If it was, it would mark the first time in her life she'd done well in science.

Dazed, she stepped back and tried to be discreet about drawing air into her lungs. It wasn't easy when all she wanted to do was gasp. She wasn't certain if she would ever breathe normally again.

It was a small price to pay for the experience.

What the hell had he been thinking, Tyler upbraided himself. He had no business kissing Brooke, no business giving in to urges he should have learned how to conquer before he'd earned the right to vote.

Saying that he couldn't help himself seemed totally unacceptable. But it was true.

"I'm sorry." He shoved his hands into his pockets, at a loss about how to repair the damage. "I'm not sure what came over me."

He was uncomfortable, she realized, and for his sake, as well as her own, she tried to laugh it off. "Obviously too much pizza. I hear the cheese affects some people that way."

His eyes searched her face. Had she felt anything? Or had he been the only one? He had no doubt that in today's society he was probably hopelessly outdated. "Then you'll accept my apology?"

"Nothing to accept." She shrugged, trying her best to seem nonchalant. "I'm as much to blame as you are. I kissed you back."

He made no comment to that, and she wasn't about to make herself crazy trying to figure out what he was thinking or feeling right at this moment. She was having enough trouble trying to sort out her own emotions.

It was time to make a getaway before she found herself initiating an encore.

"I'll send my grandmother over tomorrow for the interview, unless..." She let her sentence trail off, looking at him. Maybe this had changed everything in his eyes.

"I'd appreciate that," he answered.

He held the door for her as she slid into her car.

This was one man, she thought as she drove away, who was definitely not easy to figure out.

Chapter Eight

"Brooke, it's for you."

Murmuring something to the woman she was helping, Brooke turned and saw Heather at the rear counter, holding the telephone receiver up in the air. Turning back, she shook her head. "Take a message, Heather. I'm with a customer."

Instead of agreeing, to her surprise Heather moved up to the front register.

"I'll take your customer," her sister said. "You take the phone." There was a knowing self-satisfied smile on her face. "Trust me, you're going to want to take this one."

Now what? Brooke wondered.

"Excuse me," she said to the woman, easing herself away from the register and allowing Heather access to it. "You know, I am truly going to miss being bossed around when you go back to school."

"Not to worry," Heather called after her with a laugh. "I'll work out a schedule."

Brooke hadn't the slightest clue what the expression on Heather's face meant. Bracing herself, she picked up the receiver. "This is Brooke Carmichael, how may I help you?"

"You've already helped me, Brooke. That's why I'm calling."

Though she'd never spoken to him on the telephone before, he didn't need to identify himself. The deep rich masculine voice went right through her, making her tingle. Tyler.

She tried to make sense of what he'd just said to her. This had to be her day for being obtuse. "I'm afraid I haven't had enough coffee this morning. How did I—?"

"I've just hired your grandmother. The girls are wild about her. They wanted her to start immediately."

Brooke laughed, pleased that she had solved his problem, as well as her grandmother's.

"She does have that effect on people," Brooke agreed. Facing the front, she saw that the customer had made her purchase and left. Heather was looking at her like someone who had scored a free ticket to a spectator sport. Brooke turned her back to her sister. "Didn't I say she was wonderful?"

"You did. I'd like to express my gratitude to you for sending her my way."

Something warm curled inside of her. "You just did."

"No, I thought I could do it with something more substantial." Brooke held her breath, not knowing where this was going, afraid of following. Afraid not to. "You seem to appreciate music and I thought that perhaps you'd like to take in a concert, perhaps dinner afterward. The Boston Philharmonic is making a rare appearance at the Performing Arts Center," he added as a clincher.

Stunned, Brooke mutely held on to the receiver. Her first reaction was to say yes, but no quickly followed on its heels the second her common sense kicked in. A thousand excuses presented themselves, then melted, as flimsy as drenched rainwear made of spiderwebs.

A single thought drummed in her head. It had been a long time since she'd gone out, and she did miss enjoying herself.

Tyler interpreted her silence to mean she was searching for a delicate way to turn down the invitation. "Or if you'd rather, I could send over a dozen red roses."

The proposed concert was slipping through her fingers. Tyler Breckinridge was the first man she'd even been remotely willing to consider as a date in longer than she could remember. Brooke found her tongue. "I love roses, but a concert would be lovely."

"Wonderful." Pleasure seemed to pour into his voice. "I can pick you up at seven-thirty."

"Seven-thirty?" she echoed. He couldn't possibly mean tonight. "When?"

"Tonight."

"Tonight?" Brooke gripped the receiver in both hands, trying to steady the sudden eruption of nerves. "Isn't that a little fast?" Damn, that sounded as if she was talking about him, not the concert. "I mean, short notice? How can you get tickets so quickly?"

"Music professors have their means. I have connections," he said.

Tyler didn't add that the department chairman fortuitously happened to be the Boston Philharmonic conductor's godfather. The chairman had a block of extra tickets, two of which he'd offered to Tyler by way of a welcome-to-the-university gift.

"Ah, a man with nefarious connections. Sounds intriguing." Brooke took a breath, then plunged in. "All right, I'd love to. Let me give you my address."

"Your grandmother already took care of that." The woman had told him it was in case of an emergency, but he'd had the impression that she'd just wanted to make sure he had Brooke's address. She'd made no secret how wonderful she thought her older granddaughter was.

Instead of off-putting, it had made him faintly envious of the love that abounded within the small tight-knit family. He'd thought, when he married Gina, that he had stumbled onto something that had been, except for his younger sister, absent all during his own childhood and adolescence. He'd quickly learned that every gift came with a price.

"I see." Brooke felt color creeping up her neck. She was tempted to ask what else her grandmother had said, but was afraid of being permanently mortified by what she found out. "Remind me to take care of my grandmother."

"Please, not until next June. I need her." He smiled, thinking of the way the interview had gone. He'd made sure his daughters were present for most of it, since it was not only their welfare, but their happiness that concerned him. "She reminds the girls of their own grandmother."

"Your mother?"

"Mother-in-law." His own mother had passed away years before the girls had been born and was only a dim memory for him. Gina's mother had died only hours before Gina had, a victim of the same revenge plot.

It had to be hard for the girls, Brooke thought, moving away from friends and family. "Maybe once you're settled in, she can come out to visit them."

He realized he'd allowed himself to slip up. "That won't be possible."

His tone was quieter, darker. She wondered if he didn't get along with his late wife's mother. "That's too bad." He said nothing in response. "Invitation still stand? For the concert?" she asked.

"Yes, why wouldn't it?" He had no idea why she would think he'd suddenly changed his mind.

Honesty always worked best for her. "Because I have the distinct feeling I just put my foot into it."

The fault was his, not hers. He had to watch himself, not leave openings that invited questions and speculations about his past life. He couldn't go there, not anymore. Probably not ever. He didn't want to think what that did to the girls.

"One doesn't have anything to do with the other." Tyler realized she hadn't agreed to the time. "Seven-thirty all right?"

Brooke felt her mouth curving even as small butterflies with fledgling wings began to flutter about the pit of her stomach. "Seven-thirty is fine."

"See you then," he promised.

"See you," she echoed. The smile and the butterflies grew.

The receiver had hardly made contact with the cradle before Heather was on her like a dog on a bone it had suddenly discovered after days of deprivation. Her eyes were positively glowing in her eagerness.

"So?"

Brooke moved away from the rear counter and nonchalantly began to straighten drooping displays throughout the store. "He called to say thank-you. He's hiring Oma."

Heather followed in her wake, knowing there had to be more to it than that. "Awfully long conversation for just two words."

Taking a book that was with the wrong group,

Brooke put it where it belonged. "What were you doing—timing me?"

"More like praying for you. Did it work?" Heather caught Brooke's arm, turning her around to face her. She could read her sister's face like one of their father's much-loved storybooks. "It did. It did work. Tell me everything," Heather begged. "Where's he taking you?"

Turning away again, Brooke straightened a ghost that had become twisted. "You seem to be the one with all the conclusions. Why don't you fill in the blanks?"

Brooke was doing this to drive her crazy, Heather thought. "'Children's bookstore owner found strangled with sister's hands wrapped around her neck. Sister's actions deemed justifiable. Film at eleven.'" She presented herself in front of Brooke. "How's that?"

"About as imaginative as everything else you come up with."

There was a strange, almost foreign sensation forming within Brooke, right next to the butterflies. It took her a second to recognize it for what it was. Excitement.

Don't get carried away, she warned herself. *It's just a concert.*

Pausing, Brooke knew she wasn't going to have any peace until she gave Heather all the details. Normally she kept nothing from her sister, but she knew Heather. Heather would make a big deal out of this, and she didn't want it to be a big deal. Because if it was, she'd lose her nerve entirely and not go. It was hard to willingly get back into the swim of things after almost drowning the last time out.

"Okay, here's the whole thing. He's taking me to the concert at the Performing Arts Center." She thought of the triplets. "I guess Oma's going to be baby-sitting for him this evening."

"Tonight?" Heather's eyes widened. "My God, the man acts fast when he wants to." Heather almost said that he really had to be interested, but she knew if she did, it would spook Brooke, making her reconsider. She'd waited too long to get Brooke to this juncture to risk making a mess of it now.

Brooke could see where Heather's mind was going. "It's just to say thank-you."

Heather spread her hands innocently. "Maybe you'll find something to say thank-you about tonight, too."

"Heather."

"A customer." Heather pointed to the entrance and the woman pushing a baby carriage before her. The next moment Heather slipped away.

Where had the customer been a few minutes ago when she'd needed her to keep Heather from asking questions? Brooke thought, shaking her head.

It was like trying to pick the right outfit to wear to a disaster. She knew it was going to end up that way. Frustrated, she had more than half a mind not to go. If she *was* in her right mind, she wouldn't go, Brooke thought, exasperated.

Half her wardrobe was spread out on her bed and on every available surface in the bedroom. Going from one outfit to another, Brooke found fault in everything, as well as in her saying yes in the first place.

During the course of the rest of the day, she'd tried to keep herself too busy to think about the evening ahead. Despite a healthy influx of customers in the afternoon hours, she found that holding a moratorium on her thoughts was virtually impossible. Salvos of nerves would go off to torment her.

More than half-a-dozen times she'd made her way to the telephone to call Tyler and cancel. But each time something diverted her attention at the last moment, and she'd have to postpone making the call.

Eventually it was too late to gracefully bow out. Now if she bowed out, it would definitely have to be ungracefully.

The thought still tempted her.

Heather stuck her head in the door. The look in her eyes turned reproving. "You're not dressed yet."

"Yes, I am." Brooke looked down at herself. "These are clothes."

"Bookstore-owner clothes," Heather scoffed. Crossing to the bed, she began to deftly sift through the various articles, judging and discarding. "We need hot-babe clothes."

"That's your department, not mine." Brooke closed her eyes. What was she thinking, getting back on that dizzying merry-go-round? Just because the man kissed seductively didn't mean she had to go out with him. After a two-year dearth, given half a chance, she'd probably have thought Bugs Bunny kissed seductively. "I just want leave-me-alone clothes."

Heather spared her a look. "You're pretty much wearing them. C'mon, Brooke, it'll be fun."

"It'll be a disaster," Brooke contradicted. She flopped onto the overstuffed chair in the corner. "What am I doing? I don't remember what it's like to go out on a date."

Annoyed at what she thought sounded like defeat, Heather fisted her hands on her hips. "For goodness' sake, Brooke, it hasn't been that long. You were only married to The Rat for two years."

Heather was a lot younger than she was. Her memory tended to be fuzzy on these matters. "Yes, but I went with him for two years before that. And before that, I wasn't exactly partying every night."

Heather continued sifting and discarding. "Good news—times haven't changed all that much. You still get to be yourself on these things."

Brooke stared down at her hands. Her fingers had knotted themselves together. A companion piece for her stomach. "Well, 'myself' is nervous."

Not finding anything suitable, Heather went to the closet and continued the search. "As long as you don't spill anything on him, I'm sure he'll think 'myself' is cute."

Brooke caught her lip between her teeth. "I don't know about that…" She thought of last night. He'd looked uncomfortable when Tiffany had invited her to stay for dinner. But if that was true, why was he asking her to the concert? "He didn't strike me as someone who wants to bother dating, either."

Keeping her hand in between Brooke's dresses to mark her place, Heather glanced over her shoulder. "Well, he was the one who called, right?"

"Right."

Heather returned to her quest. "So one part of him wants to date, trust me."

Brooke laughed shortly. Easy for Heather to say. Heather had been born ready to date. It was different with her. She'd been too busy trying to be a surrogate mother to Heather during the time she should have gotten her flirting certification. "I'd rather send you."

"Sorry, I don't do stand-ins or substitutions." Heather was coming to the end of the selections and still hadn't found anything she deemed suitable. There had to be something here to make Tyler's eyes pop out, she thought. "Simon wouldn't like it and he does have a gun." She paused to wink. "Although—" Heather sighed soulfully "—it might be nice to have men dueling over me."

"Winner gets to run for the hills?" Brooke said. Heather wasn't the easiest woman to get along with, as some of her sister's dates had lamented to Brooke.

"Thanks a lot." Deciding that the perfect thing for Brooke to wear might be in *her* closet, Heather crossed to the door and went into her room. "Just for that," she called out, "when he comes, I'm trotting out your baby pictures. The naked ones."

Brooke leaned against her doorway, arms crossed. She just wouldn't go, that was all. She had nothing to wear. Heather had said so. She waited for the relief to hit. It didn't. The knot in her stomach continued tightening. "Good. He'll leave and then I won't have to go through this."

"This," Heather said, raising her voice, "is the fun part."

Couldn't tell that by her, Brooke thought. Her stomach lurched and she pressed a hand to it. It didn't help. "I think I'm going to be sick."

Coming back out of her room, looking ready for battle, Heather spoke to her sternly. "What you're going to be is terrific. What happened to the Brooke who was game for everything?"

It'd been a long time since she'd felt that way, at least about a man. They represented far too big a risk. "She lost the game, remember?"

Anger creased Heather's forehead. "Marc was the loser, not you."

Brooke looked down at her hands. At least they weren't shaking like her knees. "So why do my palms feel sweaty?"

"Humidity. Now, wear this outfit." Heather slung a turquoise version of the little black dress on her sister's arm. "With these shoes and that purse." She loaded Brooke down with the matching items she'd selected. Lucky for Brooke they wore the same size, she thought.

Brooke stared at the items that were now in her hands. "Wonderful. I'll be the most fashion-coordinated mute at the concert."

So *that* was it, Heather thought. Brooke was afraid she wouldn't have anything to talk about. She tried not to laugh. "Mute, my foot. I've never known you to lose the gift of gab, Brooke. You could talk to a stone."

"That's because stones aren't tall, dark and sexy uncalculated risks." There went her stomach again. "I was never very good at this, Heather, and I've gotten a lot worse."

Heather refused to be sympathetic. The last thing Brooke needed was someone agreeing with her. "You'll be great. Just get him to talk about himself. Guys love that. Works every time." The doorbell rang. She saw Brooke suddenly pale and cursed her former brother-in-law with her whole heart. "There he is. I'll stall him while you get dressed," Heather said.

"How about stalling him while I make my getaway?"

"I wouldn't try it if I were you," Heather warned, leaving the room. "I borrowed Simon's K-9 partner. Rufus is in the yard even as we speak, guarding the back windows."

She wasn't all that sure Heather was kidding. "One step ahead of me, aren't you?"

"Just for tonight, big sister, just for tonight." Hurrying back into the room, she gave Brooke a huge hug. "The man's dynamite, Brooke. And so are you." Stepping back, kindness filled her eyes. "And it's a concert, not a wedding. If it helps, pretend he's a little kid. Most men are, anyway." The doorbell rang again, longer this time. "Okay, dress, shoes, purse." She pointed to each as she enumerated the items. "Hurry." Leaving, Heather pulled the bedroom door shut behind her.

Brooke took a deep breath and let it out.

It amazed her that she could actually get dressed when all her fingers had suddenly turned into thumbs. But she did it, slipping on the dress and shoes, then fixing her makeup in under five minutes.

She could feel her heart racing. There was something definitely nerve-racking about going on a first date at her age. No matter what either of them called it, at bottom it was a first date. There was no other way to look at it.

She was so out of practice it was laughable. The man would bolt before the orchestra finished playing the overture.

"C'mon, Brooke," she ordered the frightened-looking woman staring back at her from the mirror. "Get a grip. It's just a few hours out of your life with a good-looking man, nothing else."

It might be a few hours, but she had a sinking feeling it was going to drag on like a life sentence.

The feeling stayed with her until she made her way to the top of the stairs and looked down.

Heather was at the foot of the staircase talking to Tyler, who looked up when he heard Brooke approach. There was no question about it. The man was bone-meltingly good-looking, even when he wasn't smiling.

And he was.

The way he looked at her when she began walking down the stairs made her feel like a debutante making her entrance at a cotillion. More than that, the appreciation in his eyes made her feel beautiful. It'd been a long time since she'd felt beautiful.

When Brooke reached the landing, Heather began to retreat. "Okay, you two don't need me around anymore. By the way, Brooke, Simon and I are going to take in the midnight movie down at the Newport Theater. Won't be back until after two." She looked pointedly at her sister, then Tyler, before withdrawing.

"Sorry about that," Brooke murmured. "She thinks she's being subtle."

He thought of his own sister and of the way they'd gotten on each other's nerves when they were still kids. A year apart, they fought like the proverbial cats and dogs. He missed her a great deal. "Nothing to be sorry about. She just wants you to be aware of the playing field."

"You sound like you speak from experience. Do you have a sister?"

"No, I don't." Opening the front door, he took her arm. "We'd better get going if we don't want to be late. Concert starts in half an hour."

If she'd been a train, Brooke would have said that she'd just been rerouted.

Chapter Nine

"**Y**ou really must know someone."

Brooke murmured the words to Tyler, careful not to let the sound of her voice interfere with the enjoyment of those around her in the darkened concert hall. They were sitting in the best seats possible for the audio and visual theater experience: fifth row, dead center.

Tyler could barely make out the hint of admiration in her voice. Brooke's voice, sultry to begin with, was so low he found himself leaning into her words in order to hear them.

And leaning into her.

Her breath slid along his cheek, registering with alarming clarity.

For one of the very few times in his life, Tyler

became oblivious to the music around him. The only thing he was aware of was the woman beside him.

He hadn't thought it would ever happen again.

Hadn't thought it possible. That disturbance of focus, that desire for another human being that was making itself so acutely felt, he hadn't thought he'd ever experience again. He'd been stunned the first time, when it had happened with Gina.

It wasn't that he had led the life of a monk, though if it had been his father's choice, he would have done nothing but eat, sleep and play music, day in, day out. A virtuoso living his life as Johnny One Note. There had been a certain irony in that. And it had never made itself clearer than it did when he met Gina. Other experiences, both of the body and the soul, paled in comparison.

He'd considered Gina his walking miracle. One miracle in a lifetime was as much as he could possibly have ever hoped for.

That it might be happening again, three thousand miles away from where his life had begun and ended, was something he was far from prepared to acknowledge. He almost felt that if he did acknowledge it, it would somehow take away from everything that Gina had been to him.

Yet here they were, feelings flowering within him just because Brooke's breath had touched his skin as she'd said something in passing.

He wondered if the past nine months had finally succeeded in making him crazy. It was one theory.

Brooke could feel his eyes on her. Goose bumps

threatened to run along her arms even before she turned to look at him. There was something in his eyes she couldn't place. "What?"

"Nothing." How could he begin to explain it to her when he couldn't even explain to himself what he was thinking, what he was feeling? At least, not in any terms he could understand and accept. "And I really can't take credit for this. The conductor's the dean's godson. Dean Anderson had extra tickets."

She tried desperately to ignore the way Tyler's voice seemed to rumble all around her like velvet thunder. "Shh," she cautioned, humor entering her voice. When all else failed, it was humor that always saw her through. "Don't explain away the magic. Just let me think you've got mysterious connections."

He inclined his head as the overture faded. "As you wish."

He sounded like a genie just then, she thought, amused. With every fiber of her being, she tried to concentrate on the entertainment before her and not the unsettling presence of the man beside her.

It wasn't easy.

Two hours and several encores later, it was over. The house lights went up and all around them was the rustling sound of people gathering their things and beginning to exit.

Brooke felt Tyler's hand at the small of her back,

guiding her from the row. Shivers emerged in the wake of his touch. She pretended they weren't there.

Reaching the end of the row, she turned toward him as they made their way out to the lobby. "I know it doesn't sound very erudite, but that just blew me away." For a second, threading her arm through his, she closed her eyes. "I could feel the kettle drums vibrating inside my chest. And the string section in that next-to-last number moved me almost to tears." She opened her eyes and saw him looking at her. For once she could read his look. Amusement. She felt herself responding even though she had no idea what was going on in his head. "What?"

"Nothing." But it *was* something. To him. A great many people claimed that this sort of music bored them. There had been several modern pieces, but for the most part, the program had comprised classical music. "I just like seeing someone enjoy music as much as I do."

Afraid he might launch into theory and execution she couldn't begin to follow, Brooke demurred. "I probably enjoy it on a much more superficial level than you do. Quite honestly I just like things that move me, that speak to me. And this did."

Tyler inclined his head to hers, hiding his smile. "I'll let you in on a secret. Beyond the professional rhetoric, that's the way the rest of us react, as well." Straightening, he winked at her as he guided her out of the building. The clusters of people scattered throughout the theater were making it difficult to maneuver. "We just couch it in more superior terms."

She hardly heard him. Her mouth had gone dry the moment she'd registered the wink. And here she thought she'd finally gotten passed her case of nerves. No such luck.

The evening was warm, serving up a sultry breeze, which intensified the way she was feeling. It took Brooke a second to find her tongue and then another second to find the words to place on it. "You're just saying that so that I don't feel inferior."

Tyler handed his ticket to an eager valet with a ponytail and an athletic torso. While the man sprinted off into the bowels of the parking structure, Tyler turned to look at Brooke. He was beginning to think that he'd find her appealing no matter what sort of light he saw her standing in. "Why would you feel inferior?"

"Because my musical knowledge isn't very extensive."

He knew that knowledge was supposed to enhance enjoyment, but there were times when too much knowledge got in the way of enjoyment. Simplicity had a great deal going for it.

Without thinking, he slipped his arm around her waist, drawing her a shade closer. "Well, anytime you feel you're lacking and would like to be filled in on something, feel free to ask." His smile rose to his eyes. "There's a fifty-fifty chance I might know the answer."

Like the ever-moving tide, some of her tension faded again. She liked the fact that he wasn't pompous about his abilities. Granted, she didn't know all that much about him, but she'd heard him play. The man would have been justified if he'd developed an unmanageable ego. Instead, he came across as a regular person, if somewhat formal. But that could very well be just his upbringing.

She looked toward the parking structure, wondering just how far in the valet had parked Tyler's car. There wasn't any sign of the black Mercedes. Brooke caught Tyler glancing at his watch. "You know, we really don't have to go to a restaurant if you want to get back to the girls."

He tried to gauge her meaning by her expression and got nowhere. "Is that your polite way of saying that you'd like the evening to end?"

Oh, God, no. Where had he gotten that idea? "No, that's my polite way of saying I know you have a lot to do and that you'd probably like to be there to tuck in the girls."

He liked the fact that she was thinking of his daughters. "Your grandmother seems capable enough to manage that monumental task."

Brooke grinned, memories tugging at her. "Oh, Oma's more than equal to it. I just thought that…well, you seemed awfully close to the girls, and—"

"I don't seem close to the girls," he corrected quietly. "I am." He moved her out of the way of a couple who were hurrying by. "Maybe part of the reason is that I'm all they have." He was aware of that every waking moment of the day and sometimes even in his dreams. For the longest time, the girls were the only reason he went on living, went on putting one foot in front of the other when all he wanted was to find his own end to the pain that was haunting him. "Having a parent die suddenly tends to make children very vulnerable."

She wasn't that removed from her own childhood not to remember. "Yes, I know."

His vehicle finally emerged in the distance. "You're talking about your father?"

"Actually my mother." Brooke looked at him. "But yes, you can add my father to that." A sadness crept over her heart as she remembered. "The day he died, I realized I wasn't anyone's little girl anymore. It hit me rather hard." She lifted one shoulder in a self-conscious shrug. "I suppose that probably sounds silly to you."

Tyler found himself fighting a very strong urge to hold her and coax back her smile. "Not really."

But then the valet pulled up in front of them and the moment disappeared.

Tyler pressed a folded bill into the younger man's hand, then got in on the driver's side as the valet held the door open for Brooke. He waited until she was in the car and buckled up. "How do you feel about French food?"

"Never met a morsel I didn't like."

Something else they had in common, he thought as he pulled away from the curb.

* * *

Because it was a weeknight, Le Fey Brigette's parking lot was not as packed as it could be, but it still took Tyler one pass down two aisles before he finally found a place to park. It was another fifteen minutes before they were seated at a table for two.

It had been a long time since Brooke had found herself sitting across from a man at such a small table.

The restaurant was cozy, with only two dining areas and a small dance floor in front of a three-piece jazz combo. Its atmosphere, served up dark and enticing, mingling with the scent of the tempting cuisine, was seductive.

As was the man sitting opposite her.

She was growing nervous again, Brooke realized. It was an absolutely absurd way for a veteran of the war between the sexes to feel. But she had earned both her medals and her scars from Marc. Like it or not, it shaded the way she looked at things.

And being alone with Tyler in these intimate surroundings made her restless. As if she was anticipating something. She couldn't decide if it was a good thing or a bad one.

The momentary silence between them was feeding her nerves. The soft music playing in the background didn't help.

She remembered Heather's parting advice. Get him to talk about himself and the rest is easy. Nothing ventured, nothing gained, she thought, watching their waitress make her way to the small attractive bar along one side.

"So, tell me something about yourself," she said. A guarded look entered Tyler's eyes. It faded when she added, "When did you first discover you liked music?"

It was safe to talk about music. While it defined him, it gave nothing away. "I didn't. Music discovered me." He cut a slice from the loaf that was left on the table and offered it to her. "It was as if I was always playing. My father was a professional musician, and there was a baby grand in the living room." He cut a piece of bread for himself. "One of his friends gave me a toy piano, thinking I might want to sit on the floor and mimic my father while he practiced."

Brooke buttered the slice generously before breaking off a piece. "How old were you?"

"Fifteen," he deadpanned. A dimple she hadn't been aware of winked on his left cheek as he grinned. "Seriously, I was probably about four at the time. But I didn't bother with the toy. I went right for the real thing."

"You could play it?" she asked.

To Tyler it was no great feat. It was merely something he had always been able to do. "I used to watch the way my father's fingers moved on the keys when he played certain songs, and I would memorize that. Then, when I was alone, I'd play back what I remembered. When my father finally caught me at it, he decided that maybe lessons were in order.''

He didn't add that at first his father had insisted on the lessons to prove to himself that his son had no real natural talent for the instrument. When it quickly became apparent that Tyler not only had natural talent but that it surpassed his father's, things became very uncomfortable and tumultuous between father and son. Until his father finally decided that this was a golden opportunity to realize all the dreams he, with his own limited talent, would never attain.

What followed was more than eighteen, tempestuous torturous years during which his father lived vicariously through Tyler's triumphs and accolades while loathing the vessel that did all the things he was not capable of doing. Peace only came on his father's deathbed.

''Did you ever think of playing professionally?'' Brooke asked. The look that came across Tyler's face made any further questions temporarily fade from her lips. He seemed to close up right before her eyes.

''Why?'' The single word cut through the air like a rapier.

The fear returned. *Had* she recognized him? It had been several years since he'd performed regularly, cutting back drastically from that sort of life when he'd married Gina. And even before then, his tours had rarely brought him to the West Coast. But she'd mentioned living in New York. There was a chance she was making some sort of connection between the person he'd been and who he was now.

He'd gone through too much to risk being recognized now.

Brooke didn't understand why her question seemed to have rattled him. It was harmless enough. "Well, you said your father played professionally, so I thought maybe you'd tried your hand at it, too."

Tyler relaxed. It was all right. "No, I never played professionally. I prefer being behind the scenes." That much at least was true. Though he'd done it only on a very limited one-to-one basis, he liked teaching, and he preferred playing for an intimate gathering than being in the center of the stage with only a spotlight for company. "It's gratifying watching someone discover music."

She'd think he would be, especially if the students had a natural aptitude. "Do the girls play?"

There'd been a time when he'd actually debated getting a second piano just to keep the peace. Bethany and Tiffany would butt heads, each trying to get sole possession of the instrument. He smiled, thinking of them. He knew they'd do it to garner his favor. As if they had to do anything more than breathe to garner it.

"Yes, to varying degrees. It's hard to get Tiffany to sit still long enough to get the fingering right, but Bethany and Stephany both play well. Especially Stephany, which surprises me."

"Why?"

"Because she seems to shy away from everything." Stephany was his little shrinking violet, his fragile flower. Born the smallest and last, she always seemed to be one step behind.

"Maybe she finds her voice in music," Brooke suggested. "Who knows? You might have a little virtuoso on your hands."

"God forbid."

He said it so vehemently he started her wondering again.

But before she could ask why he felt so strongly about one of his daughters being a virtuoso, Tyler had turned the conversation very neatly around to her. As their drinks and appetizers arrived, she found herself telling him about her life. How, like the girls, her mother had died when she was very young and she and Heather had found themselves in a single-parent home. It took no encouragement at all for her to talk about her father, a man who had both her undying love and her everlasting respect.

"He did everything," she recalled. "Oma was there to jump in whenever he had obligations to face, but I swear the man was the closest thing to Superdad the world has ever seen." She smiled fondly, pausing to take a sip of her wine. "He shifted gears in his career so he could be at home with us as much as possible. He tried so hard to make up for the fact that we lacked a mother." Looking back, she realized he hadn't so much as gone out on a date while they were growing up. Oma told her it was because he didn't want her or her sister to feel that they were being shortchanged or ignored. "Heather and I never felt the lack, I can tell you that much."

Understanding firsthand the sacrifices involved, Tyler raised his glass in a silent toast. "Sounds like a hell of a guy."

"Oh, he was, he was." Touching her glass to his, Brooke smiled at him. "I really think that the two of you would have gotten along very well."

At least they could have commiserated. Up to a point, he thought. "Oh? What makes you say that?"

That was simple. It was the reason behind her acceptance of his invitation in the first place.

"Because of the way I see you look at your daughters. There's that same determination there. You want to make everything right for them. They're very lucky to have you. And I can see that they adore you, just the way we did our dad."

"Thanks, that's nice to hear." He meant that sincerely. "There are times when I feel as if I'm groping around in the dark and making a mess of it." Tyler stopped abruptly, one brow arching as he looked at her. "We were talking about you. How did we get around to talking about me again?"

She spread her hands innocently. "Just the natural progression of things, I guess. It's called being on a date and finding things out about each other." The words echoed in her head, almost mocking her.

Cutting another slice from the loaf, he held it out to her. There was a strange look in her eye. "Anything wrong?"

Shaking her head, she passed on the bread even

though she loved it. If she ate any more, she wouldn't have room for the main course. "No, it's just that I never thought I'd catch myself dating again."

He would have thought someone like Brooke would be going out constantly. Curiosity took over. "Why? Bad experience?"

She wasn't about to ruin the evening by talking about her ill-fated marriage or the stranger she'd discovered she was married to. Instead, she shrugged and looked away. "Something like that."

It obviously bothered her. He was surprised to find that it bothered *him.* "I'm a good listener if you need someone to talk to," he offered.

"Is that a direct result of tuning the piano?" she asked, teasing.

He laughed, setting his empty shrimp-cocktail glass aside. "Well, that never hurt."

She appreciated the offer, but Marc was best left in the shadows. "Maybe someday I'll bend your ear." Provided that there was someday, she added silently. She looked down at her own shrimp cocktail. The glass was empty. It had been delicious. "You know, for a man who's new to the area, you certainly picked an excellent restaurant." Her eyes twinkled. "Or is the chef someone's godson, too?"

"I'm sure he is, but no one I know." He looked around. There were a lot of people in the restaurant, but the acoustics were such that their voices didn't carry, lending a feeling of intimacy to the meal. "The dean did suggest I might like this place."

Brooke nodded. It was an excellent suggestion. "So far, the dean is batting a thousand."

And so was she, he thought. He found himself wanting to hold her. The service was languid. It might be a while before their dinner arrived. "Care to dance?"

She couldn't remember the last time she'd danced. She only remembered how much she'd loved it while she was in college.

"I suppose you do that well, too."

He smiled into her eyes. "I don't step on feet, if that's what you mean."

"That's how I learned," she confessed. "Standing on my father's feet. I was a lot lighter then."

Probably not all that much heavier now, he judged. Tyler stood up, extending his hand to her. "Let's see how good a pupil you were." She was hesitating. "If you get stuck, I'll let you put your feet on mine and walk you through it."

She placed her hand in his. Her eyes met his. "Fair enough."

The quivering in Brooke's stomach returned, but this time, there was a happy anticipation to it.

Anticipation melted into fulfillment as Tyler took her into his arms and led her around the floor.

Chapter Ten

It was just a little after midnight when Tyler brought Brooke to her door. She hadn't intended to get home this late, but they had lingered over dinner and talked. And danced some more. Her guard had begun to lower without her realizing it until it was almost nonexistent. And somehow, time had just managed to slip away.

Brooke stood at the door, remembering what Heather had told her about being out late. Her pulse quickened as indecision ventured forward. "I had a wonderful time, Tyler."

It would have meant more, he mused, had she used his real name. The name he'd been given at birth. But Tyler was his name now, he told himself. And besides, wasn't it the man inside who counted, no matter what the name?

The trouble was, he wasn't sure who or what the man inside was anymore. Not after what he'd been through this past year. Even before Gina had been taken from him.

The only thing he knew was that whatever or whoever he was, he wanted to kiss Brooke. Kiss her and do the impossible by spending the night with her, losing himself and the thoughts that haunted him in the taste of her mouth, the feel of her body. The promise of oblivion in her eyes.

But that came at a price he couldn't afford. And it wouldn't have been fair to her, either, for she would have been giving herself to a man who didn't exist.

He might as well have asked for the moon served on fine old china.

So instead, he smiled at her, their eyes meeting, and said, "So did I."

Brooke hesitated, wondering if the question hovering on her lips would sound like an open invitation to him. Wondering if he knew what even considering the very words meant for her. A giant step outside of the world she'd been living in these past two years.

And then she heard herself asking, "Would you like to come in for some coffee, or a nightcap, or…" Her voice trailed off as her courage flagged.

God, but she did look beautiful in this light. Not the carefully made-up beauty of a model, who was the product of the right clothes and perfect makeup, but a beauty that could only be enhanced, not diminished. He couldn't resist just one touch.

His mouth curved. "Or?"

He was touching her face. Making her melt. Brooke finally found her voice. "Or some conversation."

Even as she made the offer, she knew it wouldn't be easy to deliver. It was very difficult for her to be coherent when Tyler was strumming his fingers along her face like that.

Tyler found the temptation strong. He wasn't sure how much longer he could hold his ground. He tried to erode the path by warning her. "If I come in, there won't be much conversation."

She pressed her lips together, as if that could somehow slow the pulse that seemed to have taken on a life of its own. "Comfortable silence is good, too."

There wouldn't be silence. There would be the sound of heavy breathing, of unspoken promises being broken. If he crossed the threshold into her house, it would be to make love with her. His only weapon to forestall it, for both their sakes, was the truth. Something that had become almost foreign to him.

He cupped her cheek. "So are other things." His eyes searched her face, looking for understanding. For help. "This is the first time I've felt even remotely human since my wife died, and I'm not completely sure if I want to. If I'm ready yet."

He was asking her to tell him no. To shut the door

on the evening and him. Funny, the word that would
have been so easy to utter just hours before took
effort now.

Brooke drew a deep breath. "I understand."

And oddly enough, she did. He was feeling dis-
loyal to the memory of his wife. To the grief her
passing created and to the love they had so obviously shared. It was natural and she wouldn't push.
Because if there was to be anything at all, it had to
come from him, not her.

Besides, this might all be a bad idea. A whim
created in the heat of the moment. If she looked
beyond the moment, she was feeling a little skittish
herself. Skittish about feeling this way for a man she
hardly knew. Ignorance had turned out to be her
enemy once before and had almost destroyed her.
She was afraid of a rematch.

Brooke hated the fact that that made her a coward.

In his mind Tyler blessed her for the silent support she offered. But even that only went to increase
the ambivalence within him.

There was a sweetness about her. In the midst of
all this vitality and vibrancy, there was a soft sweetness. A little, he mused, like the calm within the eye
of a hurricane. Except that she didn't wreak havoc.
Well, not exactly, anyway. For she had unsettled his
uprooted, undefined world, he could testify to that.

Testify.

The word echoed in his brain, dragging up memories too painful to deal with.

As if it could somehow help to deny them, Tyler

kissed her softly, instantly eliciting an ache within him at things that couldn't be. At least not now.

Not ever, he told himself firmly.

Or tried to.

The kiss deepened, taking him with it.

He had nothing to offer her except lies, and he had a strong suspicion that a woman like Brooke would stand only for the truth.

Something he wasn't free to offer.

Her head was spinning. How could a kiss drug and excite her at the same time? But it did.

There was passion there in his kiss, she could feel it. Passion that aroused all the dormant hungers in her that had been sleeping for so long, from the moment she'd seen Marc making love with another woman. Making love with her in their bed.

Passion erupted within her as she curled her arms around Tyler's neck. She'd thought it was all gone, evaporated. But it was alive and well and suddenly begging for more than just a kiss.

Too soon, too soon. Brooke made the break in her mind before she found the strength to carry it out physically.

She felt as if she was trembling inside as she drew away. She wasn't quite sure where she found the strength to remain standing when her knees felt like pureed cotton. Her voice took another long moment to locate. "So, I'll see you around?"

Now, leave now, before you do what you know you'll regret. He touched her face again, mentally stepping back. *Another time and place.* "I'll call you tomorrow."

Amusement mingled with the sorrow in her eyes. She knew she was doing the right thing, but right now, it felt so wrong. So empty. "Famous last words."

It wasn't a line. He didn't want it to be. Even though he knew that turning away from her was the right thing to do. "Last words only for tonight."

Her expression haunted him long after he had driven away from her door. He had no right, he told himself, to do this to her. The kindest thing would be to sever any further contact here and now before it got out of hand. Before he hurt her and himself.

Before.

He told himself he could still handle it.

The lies had reached a new height.

Unable to sleep, Brooke was drawn to the landing by the sound of the front door slowly opening and closing.

"You don't have to sneak in, you know."

In a cartoonish gesture, Heather's hand flew to her heart to keep it from leaping out of her chest.

"God, but you scared me." She hesitated. "Is he…?"

Brooke shook her head and came down the stairs, smiling. "No, he's not here. He went home."

"Oh." Disappointment surrounded the single word before a smattering of hope pushed its way through. It might not be a totally lost cause. "How soon?"

Brooke knew what she was thinking. They'd been sisters too long not to. "As soon as he brought me to my door."

"Oh." Sympathy entered Heather's green eyes. "I'm sorry it was a bad date."

It would be easier to let it go this way. If Heather thought things had gone badly, then she wouldn't ask questions. But that would be too much like lying, and she'd never lied to Heather. She wasn't about to start now.

"It wasn't. It was a very nice date."

Brooke realized she was actually using the word *date* and doing so without enduring the familiar wince in her soul. Her thoughts returned to Tyler. This man might just be the one who could help usher her back from the world of the walking wounded, after all. Tall, dark and handsome, tender and yet strong, the good professor was just about everything a woman in her right mind would want.

If she was looking for someone.

Heather was lost. "If it was such a nice date, what are you doing here alone? Why isn't he here, quickly trying to get back into his clothes before I accidentally run into him?"

Well, that had been a mistake, Brooke upbraided herself. Now she had to deal with her sister's romantic notions.

"Heather, anyone listening to you would think that you lead the kind of life they write about in those twenty-something sitcoms. Not everyone winds up in bed at the end of an evening out with a member of the opposite sex.''

''No, sometimes they do it at the end of an afternoon. I'm kidding, I'm kidding.'' Covering her head with her hands, Heather laughed as Brooke grabbed a pillow from the sofa and began hitting her with it. She looked at Brooke a little warily as her sister dropped the pillow back on the sofa. ''So, it was really nice?''

Brooke felt a smile sprouting from within her very core. She was trying hard not to dwell on it, but it wasn't easy. ''Yes, it was really nice.''

Details, Heather wanted details, but she knew Brooke. Like someone approaching a wild deer, Heather proceeded cautiously. ''When are you seeing him again?''

''I have no idea.'' Brooke went to the kitchen. Keyed up, she knew she was going to need something if she was going to get any sleep at all before she went to work. ''We didn't pledge our troth, Heather. It was just comforting to know there are some nice decent men out there.''

''Sure there are.'' Heather took a carton of milk from the refrigerator. Then, removing two glasses from the draining board in the sink, she poured a glass for Brooke and one for herself. ''It's not like Marc is the definitive example of the male of the species.'' Heather put the carton away before picking up her glass. ''There're plenty of decent men out there. I've been telling you that all along.''

Brooke sighed, setting her glass down. Warm milk would probably work better, but she couldn't bear the thought of it.

"I know that. In here." She tapped her temple. "But in here—" her hand brushed her chest above her heart "—it's another story."

"Two years is enough time for it to heal, Brooke." Now, maybe thanks to Tyler, her sister's heart was finally on the way to recovery. Heather placed an affectionate arm around Brooke's shoulders. "I'm glad you had a great time."

Brooke held up her finger. "Nice. I said nice, not great." Heather was getting carried away as it was. "Great" would have her sister issuing wedding invitations.

"Your mouth said nice, but your eyes said great." Heather began heading for the stairs, then stopped just shy of the first step to look over her shoulder. There was triumph in her eyes. "By the way, your lipstick's smeared." With that, Heather hurried up the stairs.

Brooke said nothing as she pressed her lips together. What was the point?

She could still taste him.

She told herself it didn't matter.

It had been close to a week since they'd gone out. Tyler hadn't called and it didn't matter.

But it did.

And it bothered Brooke that it did, but there was no getting away from it. For the first few days, whenever the telephone rang, whether at home or at work, her first thought was that it was Tyler. It never was. Getting annoyed and calling herself needy didn't negate the way she felt.

But by the third evening, she'd more or less gotten her feelings under control. After all, she'd had exactly what she'd wanted. A pleasant evening with no strings, no expectations and no complications.

So why did her chest have that strange unsettled achy feeling as if she'd just gone out for a marathon run without a warm-up first?

Because she had. She had no idea what she was doing, what she was experiencing. It was all jumbled.

The best thing for her, she decided, would be if he never called her again.

Now if she could just get herself to believe that.

There had never been any doubt about it. Tyler absolutely hated saying no to his daughters. Especially when they begged so earnestly.

Oh, he had misgivings. Major ones. This was going to be the first big outing he'd taken them on since before he'd found himself shouldering the responsibility of parenting on his own. Tyler knew it was a good sign that the girls were so eager about it. They were resilient, bless them, and he was eternally grateful for that. He knew that going through what they'd gone through, others might have had to see a therapist or withdrawn completely from the world into themselves. Instead, his girls continued being just the way they always had, except to be perhaps a little more loving and protective of him.

If he was going to do this, he was going to need an extra pair of eyes. Perhaps more than just one. That created a problem. A multifaceted one.

He told himself that the only reason he was calling Brooke again was because he needed her help watching the girls on the outing. He'd already asked Ada, and initially the woman had regretfully passed. It was her day for her Brownie troop.

"But maybe we could combine your girls with my Brownies," she'd suggested. "I know they'd all like to go to the fair."

He didn't want a crowd around his daughters. He wanted to be able to keep tabs on them individually. And he needed someone who could devote her attention exclusively to the triplets, not just occasionally glance in their direction. He wasn't that complacent about things yet.

So he'd told Ada never mind and found himself sitting in front of the telephone, pushing out the numbers to Brooke's store.

"Tell Mc a Story." Brooke's bright cheery voice filled the receiver the moment she picked up.

"How about the one about the music professor who found himself so immersed in classwork he forgot to call?" Tyler said.

Brooke's fingers tightened on the receiver at the same moment her muscles tightened in her stomach. "I seem to remember that one."

She was being a good sport. That made Tyler's

guilt more acute. And the apology genuine. "Brooke, I'm sorry I didn't call when I said I would."

He doesn't count, remember? Take it lightly. "You don't owe me an explanation, Tyler. Oma told me how busy you were."

Not that she had asked. Her grandmother had insisted on calling and telling her. Probably because of something Heather had said to her, Brooke suspected. It was like living inside a conspiracy.

Relieved that she wasn't annoyed, Tyler began to relax. "I have been. I hadn't realized just how much work was involved in preparing to teach."

Confused, Brooke frowned. "I thought you said you taught before."

Damn. He just wasn't any good at this lying business. "Every place is different." It was a poor excuse, but it was the only thing he could think of.

She supposed that was true enough. Brooke nodded at the customer coming in with three blond boys, all under the age of six. How did these parents manage? she wondered.

"So, how's it going?" Brooke asked Tyler. There was silence, as if he didn't know what she was referring to. "Preparing for classes," she added.

He glanced at the books scattered throughout the small den. "All right. I'm beginning to smooth out the rough spots."

"And the girls? Oma tells me they're as lively as ever."

"They are. They're the reason I'm calling you."

That didn't come out right, he realized. But he didn't want to mislead her. He wasn't calling her because she'd lingered on his mind all week, wasn't calling her because he desperately wanted to see her again, alone. It wouldn't be fair to let her know that. One of them dealing with the problem was more than enough.

It was Saturday and Brooke knew Oma was busy elsewhere. "Did something happen to the girls?"

"No," he said quickly, then fumbled for the right words. "But, well, I realize this is short notice, but the university is holding a fair on the grounds today and tomorrow, and the girls are dying to attend."

She wasn't sure where this was going. Was he too swamped with preparations to go to the fair? "You want me to take them?"

Relieved that this had been easier than he'd anticipated, he didn't really hear the words. "You wouldn't mind?"

"Why should I mind?" She realized she'd missed seeing the triplets. "I like your daughters, Tyler. They're sweet and very entertaining."

"When are you free?"

Since she was taking his daughters, there was no need to pretend she was busy. "Well, Heather's here at the store today and I've hired a part-time sales-clerk to help out, too, so technically, I could take off now if I wanted to. I am the boss."

"Great." His personal schedule had already been shot to hell. He knew he wasn't going to have any peace until he gave in to his daughters. "We can pick you up in an hour."

"'We?'" she echoed in surprise. "You're coming, too?"

He didn't understand why that surprised her. Hadn't he made himself clear? "Sure, why not?"

She shrugged, though she knew he couldn't see her. Brooke dragged a hand through her hair and caught Heather looking at her. She turned her body away so Heather couldn't practice her lip-reading skills. "I was under the impression that you were asking me to take them for you, not with you."

He knew it had been too easy. "Why, does this change things?"

For half a second, she had the urge to run. With effort, Brooke squelched the feeling. "Yes. It makes it nicer." *Congratulations. Another giant step for Brooke Carmichael.*

"I bet you say that to all the music professors." God, was that him flirting? he wondered. What had come over him?

And then she laughed and he knew what had come over him, but refused to recognize it for what it was.

"Only the ones who have triplets and forget the meaning of the word 'tomorrow.'" She blew out a breath. "Sorry, just had to get that in. I'm okay now. It's out of my system."

He heard himself laughing. It felt good. "That's all right, I deserved that and more. Will one hour be enough time for you?"

"Depends."

"On what?"

"On whether you just want me to join you or put the actual fair together." Heather had come around the counter and was looking at her, one brow raised in a serious question. She had no choice but to nod and was only grateful that Heather hadn't cheered out loud but had contented herself with a mere arm-pumping action.

He'd been right in his estimation. The woman was a dynamo. "Joining us will be enough. From what I hear, the fair is already fully assembled. See you at your place in an hour."

"I'll be waiting." Brooke felt her mouth curving into a smile at the words.

Tyler rose from behind his desk and caught his reflection in the window. The near transparent face that looked back at him was smiling broadly.

The next moment he was besieged on three sides by his daughters. They'd been listening at the door. Why didn't that surprise him?

His arms went out, drawing all three close, knowing there would come a time when moments like this would be only in his memory. He absorbed them now.

"Yes, we're going to the fair. And yes, Brooke is coming with us," he told them, anticipating their questions.

He also anticipated the cheer that went up. Mostly because he felt like cheering himself.

* * *

"I'm really glad you decided to come along." It was dark and Tyler's arms were filled with children. Specifically two. He was carrying Stephany and Bethany while Brooke held Tiffany in her arms. Worn-out by more than half a day at the university fair, the girls had all fallen asleep within minutes of one another.

Brooke laughed softly as they reached his car. "You're only saying that because you couldn't figure out how to grow an extra set of arms to carry all three of them yourself."

"Well, yes, there's that," he agreed, his mouth quirking in amusement. Careful not to wake either daughter, he stooped and inserted his key into the car-door lock, turning it. "And because I didn't want you to think I was avoiding you."

"Never crossed my mind." Shifting Tiffany, she opened the rear door for Tyler and moved back as he placed his daughters inside. "Well, okay, it crossed it, but I didn't dwell on it." She surrendered Tiffany to him. "Oma said you were busy and, anyway—" she shrugged "—it's only been a few days."

Straightening, he looked at her. "Six," he corrected.

So he knew. She tried to look as if the number was a surprise to her. "Been counting?"

"Yes, I have." He shouldn't have been, he thought, but he was.

With all three girls safely inside his car, leaning against one another like pretty little rag dolls arranged on a bed, Tyler felt it safe to steal a moment for himself. As safe as it could be, given that he was most definitely playing with fire and ill equipped to put out the blaze he was afraid might result.

He took Brooke into his arms and kissed her, anyway.

And missed the gleeful wink exchanged among his sleepy contented daughters.

Chapter Eleven

Head spinning, body aching for more, Brooke forced herself to take a step away from Tyler. But all the breathing room in the world wasn't going to calm her system anytime soon.

Still, she summoned a smile to cover the turmoil he'd just caused and looked at him. "Better be careful where you do your kissing, Professor, or you're just liable to get a reputation."

He knew she was right. That had been a misstep on his part. Still, Tyler couldn't quite get himself to get into his car and his role as Daddy just yet. He wanted to linger with her a moment longer. "What kind of a reputation?"

This time the smile was not coaxed or summoned. This time it came from within. "The kind that labels you the new, sexy professor in the Music Department.'' She held up her hands before her as if framing a scene. ''I can just see it now. Next registration, there'll be a stampede of young, highly impressionable and quite probably fairly experienced female students who've suddenly decided that they just adore music theory and have a crying need to learn everything they possibly can about it—as long as you're the one who'll be doing the teaching.''

He laughed at the outlandish scenario. ''I sincerely doubt that.''

He did, she realized. The man obviously shaved without looking into the mirror. ''If you do, then you haven't spent much time around just-turned-legal young women.''

His experience with women was limited in range. The women in the world he'd occupied before Gina had come into his life, other than his sister, were predominantly of the older, sophisticated variety who spent their time between fund-raisers seeking a way out of boredom. He'd had his first sexual experience at fifteen with an insatiable dark-haired socialite twelve years his senior.

Yet with all her appetites, she suffered in comparison to the woman in front of him now.

Tyler toyed with Brooke's hair. ''Actually no.''

Something wasn't jibing, although when he was this close to her, it was hard for her to think straight. ''Then you taught in a high school?''

The question caught him off guard. ''What?''

''Well, if you haven't been around female students ages eighteen and upward, you had to have taught in high school.''

He'd never actually nailed down the story that was to be his background. He'd never really had to before. For one reason or another, whether it was because he'd been filled in by someone in the government or actually strapped for a professor, the department head had never questioned him about his past experience. It had just been tacitly assumed.

''Part of the time.''

That was an odd answer, she thought. She wanted to ask him the names of the schools where he'd taught, but was afraid that sounded too much like an interrogation. So she settled for a vague question, instead. ''And the rest of the time?''

He dropped his hands. ''I just didn't mingle.'' Tyler opened the front passenger door for her. ''Maybe we should get going,'' he suggested, rounding the front of the vehicle to the driver's side.

The switch in conversation was so abrupt she didn't say anything for a moment.

''Okay,'' she agreed quietly, getting into the car.

She supposed he didn't care to have people prying, but after that kiss, she hadn't thought of herself as just *people*.

Maybe, Brooke told herself tersely, she needed to rethink things before her insides got so scrambled she couldn't think anymore.

He tried to stay away from her, he really did.

It was one of the first failures of his life.

On the surface there was certainly enough to keep him occupied, both mind and body. The new quarter stretched before him, ten weeks with a host of classes scattered between the hours of nine to five over a four-day period, leaving Fridays to grade papers, to prepare lessons and to plan. And, of course, there were the girls with questions and stories and fears to allay.

But thoughts of Brooke crept in, anyway, finding tiny fissures to sneak through and widen until all that was on his mind was her. It didn't help that his daughters talked about her incessantly and that Ada could be counted on to add her two cents at the drop of a hat. More than once he'd heard Ada declare how something one of the girls did reminded her so much of something Brooke had done at their age.

It was as if Brooke was constantly there, in spirit, if not in form.

He felt like a man fighting a battle and the only one really losing was him.

Because the girls mentioned her so often, repeatedly asking when she would be back, there was no way he could turn a deaf ear and, after a while, no reason to. There was no doubt Brooke was good with them and to them.

There was also no doubt that he missed seeing her as much as they did.

Perhaps even more so.

He lasted a little more than a week before the excuses he'd been handing himself became old and laughable. The following Tuesday, during a midmorning break, he found himself tapping out Brooke's telephone number on his office keypad.

He knew all about why this was wrong, why he shouldn't be giving in to his feelings. But the very fact that Brooke had regenerated these feelings was the reason he was calling. He needed to believe that he was more than just a walking shell.

All week long, Brooke Carmichael had been playing along the recesses of his mind like a melody that defined his life. A melody that refused to fade away. He knew there were consequences for humming the tune, but he stubbornly put off thinking about them, telling himself that he had a long way to go before he reached a dangerous juncture.

"Tell Me a Story," Brooke answered the phone.

This time, no quick comeback came to him. Only an apology for taking so long to call. But he knew she didn't want to hear excuses. He didn't waste either of their time. "Brooke, it's Tyler."

"Yes, I know."

That took him aback. Even he hadn't known he was going to call her until just now. "How?" And then it came to him. "Caller ID?"

She laughed. She'd noticed the one time she'd been at his house that he had a caller ID box near his telephone, but she saw no need of the device herself. "Better. Woman's intuition."

"Oh." He smiled to himself, rocking back in his chair. The explanation made her sound even more feminine. "And has your woman's intuition told you why I'm calling?"

"Well, it has either something to do with the girls or you." Cradling the telephone against her ear, she rung up the book a customer handed her, smiling at the little boy beside his mother.

"Very clever." He stopped rocking and leaned forward. He didn't realize he was holding his breath until he released it. "Busy tonight?"

She thought of the lists lying on the desk in the rear. Long lists of books with blank spaces beside them. Blank spaces that had to be filled in and should have been done yesterday.

"As a matter of fact, I am." Brooke didn't bother keeping the regret she felt out of her voice. Placing the slim volume in a bag with the receipt, she handed it to the customer. "I have inventory to do. I'm behind as it is, and I'm going to be helpless."

"Helpless?" He couldn't picture her like that.

"As in, without help. Heather is currently immersed in the mad scramble of the second week of classes, and my new hire just quit this morning." Brooke made a mental note to call the temp agency, but it wouldn't do her any good tonight. "Something about finding herself. Her boyfriend just decided to pick up and go to another state, and she's going with him. I guess they'll both find themselves in New Mexico," she said philosophically. There was no point agonizing over how shorthanded this left her. She'd been through worse.

Tyler paused, debating. "Exactly what's involved in a bookstore inventory?"

Something she definitely wasn't looking forward

to, she thought. There weren't many things she put off, but doing the inventory was one of them. "Crossed eyes mostly, from reading names on lists and checking them against what's on the shelves and in the back storeroom."

Tyler wanted to see her tonight. It didn't matter in what surroundings or in what circumstances. "Need help?"

"God, yes, I..." She stopped dragging her hand through her hair—an unconscious gesture of frustration—as his words registered. "Are you volunteering?"

He wondered if maybe he was letting himself in for more than he bargained for. But there was no rescinding the offer now. "Well, I was going to suggest seeing a new play being put on by this little theater group I've just heard about, but taking inventory sounds as if it might be interesting."

Brooke laughed. He wanted to see her. She felt as if a long string of warm lights had just been turned on inside her. Although she warned herself that she'd gotten hurt the last time she let down her guard with a man, Brooke wanted to enjoy a tiny interlude with Tyler, who raised her pulse just by breathing in the same vicinity. "You obviously have a low threshold when it comes to interesting."

"Try me."

The words rippled against her ear. Stifling a shiver, Brooke let out a long shaky breath and hoped he didn't hear. "Sounds like you're making me an offer I can't refuse."

There was a student knocking on his door. Tyler straightened in his chair. He waved the young man in. "I'd like to think that."

"You're on." She hoped that sounded more nonchalant than she felt. "Bring your glasses. I'll be here all evening."

"Will do."

Hanging up, Brooke hugged herself. A second later she realized she wasn't alone but was being closely observed by a short person of no more than five. It looked as if morning kindergarten had let out.

"Always remember to like yourself," she told the little boy in a low whisper.

The boy nodded solemnly at the advice.

She was all set to think that he had either forgotten or, more likely, thought better of the venture and found someone else to go with to the play. When she heard his light knock right above the Closed sign on her glass door, her heart leapt into her throat.

A fine way for a woman of twenty-seven to act, she admonished herself. But she couldn't seem to slow her feet as she hurried to the door to unlock it. Carelessly nonchalant just didn't seem like an apt description when it came to anything to do with this man.

Tyler walked in and immediately seemed to fill the shop. She looked around the mall corridor before locking the door again. "Where are the girls?" She'd half expected them to be with him.

"With your grandmother." Was it his imagination, or did the empty store with its dimmed lighting seem strangely romantic? "Ada couldn't volunteer her services fast enough when I told her I was helping you with your inventory." He smiled. "I think she misinterpreted what I meant."

"No doubt." Brooke sighed. One way or another, Oma never stopped matchmaking. "Don't worry, I'll set her straight." Brooke picked up the lists she'd dropped on the counter when he'd knocked. "Oma is probably the world's greatest romantic." According to Oma, the world belonged in couples. And you kept trying until you got a thing right. Her divorce meant nothing to Oma. It was merely a temporary setback in the scheme of things. "She keeps seeing gentlemen callers in the shadows where there are none."

Following her to the rear of the store, Tyler couldn't help noticing the sway of her hips. He'd always been a sucker for rhythm. "Gentlemen callers?"

She looked at him over her shoulder. "Sorry, I just rediscovered *The Glass Menagerie* for about the twentieth time."

Interested, Tyler crossed his arms. "So, children's books are not the only thing that take up your time."

"Sometimes it feels that way," she admitted, "but no, I love a good mystery, a good play, a good romance. Just about a good anything." Brooke was suddenly aware that sounded like an outright invitation. "As long as there are pages involved," she added. "I love to read. How about you?"

"I used to." Getting lost in words had been his one escape from the rigorous demands of his schedule. Because the work was as taxing to him mentally as the work any field laborer endured, escape was necessary. "But now my mind wanders."

She waved away his words. "You're too young to have a wandering mind."

He looked around all the shelves and wondered if she meant to count each book housed on them. It seemed like a monumental task. "It's not a function of age. It's a byproduct of how much you have on your mind. And, anyway, sometimes I feel as if I'm at least 157."

Brooke pretended to take slow measure of him and became tangled up in her own charade. He was wearing jeans and a tan-and-blue-striped short-sleeved pullover that adhered to every ripple on his upper torso. The only way the man could have gotten muscles like that was if he bench-pressed pianos, instead of just played them.

The moisture in her mouth vanished. She reached for the remainder of her last can of diet soda on the counter. "Well, for 157, you're in amazingly good shape."

Because he had a sudden thirst, he inclined his head at the can she held in a silent question. "You're just saying that because you want me to move boxes."

"No." She surrendered the can. "I've seen how you move boxes—you don't." She couldn't help being aware that his lips had just touched the can where hers had been a moment earlier. Brooke told herself she was going through her second adolescence a great deal faster than she'd thought she would. "Besides, inventory doesn't involve moving, at least not boxes. It involves counting." The corners of her mouth rose. "You can count, can't you?"

He never cracked a smile. "Only up to the amount of fingers and toes I have."

"Then you're in luck." She threw open the door to the small office/storage area. They might as well start here and work their way out. "I usually don't stock more than twenty copies of a single title. Any more is not really profitable when it comes to children's books."

He didn't know the first thing about the book market, children's or otherwise. "Not even the Willie Wanderer series?"

She shook her head. "Not even the Willie Wanderer series." That was why her father had written as many as he had, combining both quality and quantity, not an easy feat.

Tyler looked around the area with renewed interest. "Learn something every day."

She liked the fact that he seemed interested in what she did for a living. Or that at least he went through the motions of showing interest. Conversations with Marc had always centered on what he was doing, even when they'd begun by talking about her day. "That's what keeps you fresh."

His eyes captured hers and suddenly the lightness

vanished. "And what keeps you fresh, Brooke Car-michael?"

It took her a second to find her tongue. She'd thought she'd swallowed it. "Work."

He believed her. "We have that in common." There were times when the only thing that kept him sane were the notes in his head.

If she stood here, looking at him like this, she was going to kiss him. And then nothing would get done. Abruptly she reached for a pencil and handed it and an inventory page to him. "Okay, let's get started."

He saluted with the eraser part of the pencil. "You're the boss."

"Brooke, where are you?"

Slipping into oblivion, she thought. Paraphrasing one of her favorite lines from *The Wizard of Oz,* she raised her voice and called out, "Please pay attention to the woman behind the stacks."

That was just the trouble, he thought, walking to the rear of the store—he was. Perhaps paying a little too much attention, and it was causing him to lose his ordinarily steely focus.

He found her sitting in the large rocking chair that she'd told him had once been her father's. It all but dominated the small back room, which did double duty as an office and a storage area for both incoming books and those that had worn out their welcome on the shelves but she couldn't bring herself to mail back. He liked that about her. She had a soft heart.

"Here." He handed her a tall covered container of diet soda. There was a straw peeking out of a hole he'd just punched. "I had a hell of a time convincing the guy who was closing up that he wanted to sell these to me." He pushed his own straw through the plastic top. "Fortunately he was smaller than I was."

She let the first long sip settle in. God, but she had been thirsty. Brooke raised her eyes to his. "You, a bully? I don't believe it."

"Thirst makes a man do unexpected things sometimes." And not, he thought, his eyes sweeping over her slowly, just simple thirst involving beverages. "Besides, I knew how much you needed this."

He had that right. Inventory was thirsty work. "You're a saint," she said with a sigh, consuming nearly half of the extra-large container.

"Just an empath at times," he amended. Looking around, he realized for the first time that there was only one chair in the place. "I guess you don't usually entertain company here."

"I hardly entertain *me* here." Rising to her feet, she gestured at the swaying rocker. "Go ahead, sit. You've earned it."

He made no move toward it. "It's not polite to sit when a lady's standing."

She began to protest that he was being silly, then stopped. "This is like that old Aesop's fable about the father and son who were taking a mule to market."

He was completely unfamiliar with fables of any

kind. No one had ever read to him as a child, and his girls all favored stories with at least one princess in them. "Must have missed that one."

Leaning a hip against the cluttered desk, she began the short tale. "Well, there's this father and son going to sell their donkey—"

"I thought it was a mule," he teased.

Amusement tugged at her lips. "Whatever. You want to hear this or not?"

He made no effort to hide his smile. "I'm all ears."

"When they're both walking beside it, a passerby ridicules them for letting the animal go to waste. When the boy rides it, another passerby says he's being disrespectful of his father, that the old man should ride. They trade places and the father gets on the mule, but then another passerby says that he's lazy and ignoring his duty as a father."

Finishing his soda, Tyler put the empty container on a corner of the desk. "Seems to me there's an awful lot of busybodies in this village. I suppose then they both try to ride it."

He was getting the hang of this. She grinned. "They do."

"And what's the criticism then?"

"That it puts a strain on the mule."

"Figures." Tyler looked thoughtfully at the rocking chair. "I don't think the chair will complain, though." He surprised her by sitting down and then holding his arm out to her, as if waiting for her to join him. "Want to try?"

She was about to demur. She didn't know why she didn't. Brooke felt her heart hammering as she set her drink down on the desk.

Telling herself she was being silly made no difference. Her heart continued hammering in double time.

The man was just tired, that was all. And polite.

Still, she held her breath as she slowly lowered herself onto his lap.

A warmth began to curl through his chest. He inclined his head toward hers. Her perfume filled his senses, making him just the slightest bit dizzy.

"I don't think you'll weigh any more if you breathe," he confided.

Brooke released the breath she was holding. "Probably not."

Closing his arm around her seemed only natural. And right. "You know, I've been to concerts, to performance theater and some pretty unusual things, but I've never been to an inventory before."

Brooke felt like curling up on his lap like a contented kitten. She fought the feeling. Complacency had been her downfall before. If she wasn't alert, she wouldn't see things coming at her. "How do you like it?" she asked.

"It has its moments."

His eyes were touching her. Caressing her. Breathing became an issue again for Brooke. "Such as?" she asked.

"Such as now," he whispered softly. And then

he ran his knuckles along her cheek. "I want to kiss you, Brooke."

Her pulse quickened. She struggled to sound natural. "Are you serving notice?"

His eyes never left hers. He could spot fear if he saw it. If he saw it in her eyes, he would back away. "Warning you."

"Why?" She could almost taste the question. Anticipate the answer. "Is this kiss going to be different?"

He didn't answer her one way or another. Not verbally.

He showed her, instead.

Gathering her into his arms so that she was as close to him as his own heartbeat, Tyler brought his mouth down on hers. And in that instant brought all the remaining walls around her crashing down.

It happened so quickly she couldn't have been able to clearly trace the progression if she tried. One moment she was on Tyler's lap, her mouth sealed to his, her soul crying out in wonder and excitement. The next they were both on their feet, their bodies melding.

Her head was spinning as his hands passed over her body. Never mind that there was clothing in the way. Never mind that the tiny room was windowless and close to airless. Never mind that there were piles of children's books bearing witness to the complete and utter meltdown occurring within her.

She wanted this moment. Now.

Chapter Twelve

It was wrong, but he lacked the strength to walk away. It had been drained from him. Drained away and substituted with a desire so intense he didn't think he could breathe without giving in to it.

One taste of her lips was too much. A thousand nights of lovemaking wouldn't have been enough.

The thought resounded in his brain as he pressed his mouth to hers again.

He could feel his body igniting from wanting her. It did no good to deny this moment, to say that there was too much in the way to ever make what was happening, what he was doing, right.

But none of that mattered right now.

All that mattered was kissing her, having her. Making love with her.

Tyler had never thought of himself as a particularly physical man. For as long as he could remember, things of the soul, of the mind, had always meant more to him than pleasures of the flesh. One was lasting, the other as fleeting as daylight.

Yet fleeting or not, it held him in its grip, and he was giving himself up to this tremendous appetite because he had no choice.

He needed this.

Needed her.

Heart pounding like a tribal drum announcing a sacred ritual, his lips raced along her face, her neck, the swell of her breasts. Feverishly he worked to clear away the obstacles the layers of clothing created. He wanted to touch her, to feel her and for a moment, just one moment, pretend he was nothing more than a man making love to a woman. A woman who had come so quickly to matter.

He could feel her trembling as his fingertips brushed her body, trembling as he opened buttons, pulled out edges of fabric from waistbands and tested the limits of confining garments.

He scarcely recognized himself. Didn't recognize himself.

It didn't matter.

This wasn't like her, and yet it was more like her than anything else she'd ever done. It was as if everything else in her life had been leading to this single moment in time, as if she were shedding some ponderous cocoon and finally able to lift her wings to the wind and fly.

She felt drugged and incredibly lucid at the same time. The small room slipped into a haze, yet other things she perceived as clearly as crystal. The look in his eyes, the touch of his hand. The scent of desire.

Sensations came at her from all directions, threatening to overwhelm her as they met and battled for possession of her soul.

Her body quickened and her fingertips faltered as she tugged on clothing that refused to cooperate, a belt buckle whose clasp was slow to release. Her body heated from the warmth of his gaze on her. She wanted him to be as bare as she, as exposed as she. She wanted them to be equal in this strange new place they had ventured into together. If she was disoriented, she wanted the same for him. If her head swam, then so should his. And if her soul felt suddenly unshackled, she wanted that for him, too.

Equality in passion. It would make for a hell of a slogan, she thought thickly.

In the midst of the swirling haze engulfing her, Brooke heard his voice, deep, rich, low, murmuring in her ear. Dancing along her skin. Focusing, she realized that he wasn't whispering terms of endearment. It was a question. One that made both the moment and him that much dearer.

"Are you sure?"

Standing there in only her underwear, with the lone gooseneck lamp on the cluttered desk lighting the room, it took her a second to realize what he was asking. She could feel her body quivering with anticipation.

"Too late to fill out a questionnaire form now," she breathed.

The slope of her shoulder was sweet and he had to struggle not to lose himself in the taste of her skin. Struggle not to lose himself in the frenzy whirling through him, seeking possession.

Drawing his head back, he looked into her eyes. "It's never too late."

The words were difficult to utter. Not only because excitement and anticipation had stolen his breath, but because one word from her would rob him of what he wanted most at this moment in time. But there was nothing in the world, not even his own cravings, that would cause him to impose his will on her. To bend her to his desire. He needed to know she wanted it as much as he did. Or, since that wasn't possible, almost as much.

There would be enough regrets later. He didn't want this to be part of it.

"Oh, yes it is," she whispered.

It was too late for her. Too late to turn back. And much too late to want to.

Taking his face in her hands, she pressed her lips to his, making him forget what he was going to say next, making him forget whatever ragged thought had torn itself away from the fabric of desire and tried to present itself to him.

He couldn't think, couldn't talk. All he could do

was react. To himself, to her, to things he'd thought long faded from his life.

Stripped of her clothes, she twined her body around his. Her skin was like soft clean sheets of blank paper, waiting for the first note to be composed and written down. Preserved for all time.

It excited him just to touch her, to anticipate the next pass of his fingers.

His own clothing lying in a jumbled heap against hers, Tyler gently laid her down on the floor.

She sank beneath waves of warm passionate kisses that came one after the other until her knees buckled and her arms turned to softened butter with only enough strength left for her to wrap them around his neck.

She couldn't get enough of him.

His kisses spread from her lips to her face to her throat, then circled her breasts where her heart was beating wildly for him.

The fire that was stoked within her demanded movement, demanded repayment. Arching against his touch, she tangled her hands in his hair and brought his mouth back to hers. Sealing her body to his. Kissing the last of him senseless.

And when he came to her, her body ripe with wanting, primed for him, he did it not with the urgency that she remembered Marc showing. Instead, the hurricane turned into poetry. Joining his hands with hers, lifting them up over her head, Tyler moved slowly, purposefully, as if anything quicker would somehow lose her within its own gratification.

He wanted to give her pleasure, to make the regrets she could and would have be mitigated by the sensations that she had experienced in return for giving him this most precious of gifts. Herself.

When he felt her legs wrapping around him, heard the muffled cry against his shoulder, he knew he had succeeded in bringing her to the highest peak. He hastened to join her so they could be together at the final stop in their journey.

Arrival came with a thunderclap that echoed in his head as it drenched his body in sweat.

Exhausted, spent, he felt the euphoria, the madness beginning to recede. Tyler held on to it as long as he could.

Mentally he made his apologies to Gina, but in his heart he knew she would have understood. She wouldn't have wanted him to remain an empty shell of a man for the rest of his life. She would have wanted him to try to find happiness, just as he would have wanted the same for her had their situation been reversed.

But what he wanted didn't count now.

What he had done did.

Slowly shifting, he moved his weight from Brooke onto his elbows and looked down at her. Her eyes were still closed. Her makeup was gone. He found her more beautiful now than before.

Drawing in a breath, he tried to gather himself together. She stirred beneath him. He smiled down at her face. "So, is this how you usually conduct your inventory?"

"No, this is a first." Biting back an almost giddy grin, she met his gaze. "I may never be able to look at another copy of *The Lost Kitten* the same way again."

When he raised a quizzical brow, she pointed to the poster just behind him, right above her desk. On it was a black-and-white kitten, clearly frightened, picking its way through a dense forest from the shadows of which peered dark malevolent eyes.

Turning to look at it, Tyler laughed. There was little space there on the floor next to her desk. He made himself comfortable beside her as best he could, gathering Brooke to him with his arm. For a moment there was just the sound of their breathing. He stared at the dark ceiling.

"I want you to know I didn't plan this," he said.

Brooke blew out a breath and wondered if her heart was ever going to get back to normal, or if she was doomed to have one that felt as if it belonged to an overenergized hummingbird.

"You couldn't have. Nobody could have." She raised herself on her elbow to look at him. The ends of her hair teased his chest. The feel of her soft breasts against his side made his gut tighten again. "And I want you to know that I'm not the kind of woman who usually makes love on the first inventory."

Tyler could feel the laughter bubbling up inside

of him. The lady was something else. "I didn't think you were."

With all his heart, he wished that things were as simple as she was making them sound. That his life was only as complicated as she thought it was. He sighed. Wishing wouldn't make it so, but he could push back consequences for a little while.

She was still looking at him, still stirring him. He cupped her cheek in the palm of his hand. "Are we finished?"

A grin nothing short of wicked curved her mouth. "I'd say that was up to you."

He laughed. He knew he should get up, but he liked being here this way with her. Having her to himself. Pretending that nothing else existed beyond this small perimeter. "I mean with the inventory."

"Oh, yes, that's finished." The papers were all neatly put away in a folder in her desk. "Thanks to you."

It was too late to make the play performance at the theater, but they could still get something to eat at a nearby restaurant. "Hungry?"

She tried to remember when she'd last eaten. Memories of an unappealing sandwich at around eleven flitted through her head. She could feel her stomach suddenly protesting. Lovemaking burned up calories. She nodded. "Starved."

He toyed with her hair, running the ends through his fingers. Silky, he mused. Like her body. "How does pizza sound?"

"Wonderful." She moved closer to him. The look

that came into his eyes wasn't lost on her. "Can we get take-out and bring it home to the girls?" Leaning back, she angled her watch, trying to catch the light. "What time is it, anyway?"

That she could think of his daughters at a time like this made his heart swell even as his guilt over the lies he'd told her intensified. With his last bit of resolve, he squelched those thoughts.

"Time to kiss you again." Even as he said it, he bracketed her hips with his hands, shifting her onto him. Her body heat penetrated his. He raised his head, snaring her lips.

It was a while before they got around to ordering the pizza.

Heather was beginning to worry. Brooke was never this late coming home from the store, even on the days she did inventory. She paused over the statistical-anthropology book she was suffering through and debated calling Simon to check the mall for her. Heather was in no hurry to call him, seeing as how they were both smarting from a pretty nasty argument. He'd started becoming possessive, and that was her signal to back away.

She liked her freedom just fine.

It wasn't in her nature to worry, but Brooke was so dependable that clocks could be set by her comings and goings. Brooke didn't make a break in routine without announcing it.

Something was up. Trying not to let her imagination run away with her, Heather reached for the telephone just as she heard the front door open and then close again.

Finally.

She let out a breath and then did her best to look as if she was oblivious to the time. Burying her nose in her book, she casually glanced up in time to see Brooke enter the kitchen.

"Hi, I saved you some dinner," Heather said.

"Thanks, I already ate." Brooke and Tyler had finally gotten around to placing the order for pizza. The delivery boy arrived with two large pies just after they'd pulled into Tyler's driveway. Oma had stayed long enough to have three slices. The girls had fallen asleep listening to her read them a story about Willie's adventures.

Brooke was beginning to entertain the idea of maybe writing a Willie adventure of her own.

Heather had promised herself that she wasn't going to say anything about the time, but she couldn't help herself. "Find a few books you didn't know you had?"

Brooke blinked, realizing she was standing in the middle of the room, daydreaming. Or was that nightdreaming? It didn't matter. Nothing mattered but the beautiful glow she felt.

"Why?"

"Well, I know you were stuck doing inventory tonight and you're home so late, but you seem happy—" Glancing up, Heather stopped pretending she was reading. And then she saw it. That telltale glow. "Oh, my God, you got some, didn't you?"

''Some?'' Flustered, Brooke felt her cheek, as if there was a mark on it that she could wipe away. ''Some what?''

''Some,'' Heather repeated, drawing the word out as if the extra time she gave it would somehow allow the word to penetrate her sister's consciousness and make her realize what she was referring to.

Heather rose from the table and nearly overturned her chair. She crossed to Brooke, studying her sister's face intently.

She wasn't wrong.

''Who…?'' It came to Heather as quickly as lightning. ''The professor! You saw the professor tonight, didn't you?'' Heather asked.

Brooke shrugged carelessly and avoided her sister's eyes. ''He came to help with inventory.''

''And you did it right there in the store? Wow.'' Because Brooke turned from her and opened the refrigerator, Heather shifted around so that she could get a better look at her face. Admiration shone in her eyes. ''You're gutsier than I thought.''

Brooke reached for a glass, not really aware of what she was doing. ''Heather, I don't know what you're talking about. Where else would we do inventory but in the store?''

Grinning, Heather took the glass out of Brooke's hand and pulled her into the hallway. Standing behind her, she turned Brooke so that she was facing the mirror on the wall.

''There.'' Heather pointed to the reflection. ''That's what I'm talking about. The stars in your eyes, the rosy glow of your cheeks—'' Heather took a closer look at Brooke's neck ''—and what looks like possibly the beginnings of a hickey on your neck.''

Fighting off embarrassment, Brooke raised her hand to the spot, covering it. ''That's a bite from a paper mite.''

''Is that what you call him?'' Heather made no effort to wipe amusement from her face. ''Strange term of endearment, but hey, you were never normal when it came to anything.''

''Stop that,'' Brooke said, and walked back into the kitchen.

''Okay, I will, but don't you.'' Heather grinned, following Brooke. ''Happiness looks good on you, Brooke,'' she said, sitting back down at the table again. ''I haven't seen you looking like this for too long.''

Brooke slanted a look at her. ''You're letting your imagination run away with you.''

Unable to resist, Heather got up as Brooke walked passed her and hugged her hard. ''Sorry, you've just made me so happy. So, what do I call him now?'' She released Brooke. ''Tyler? Ty? Tiger?'' Her lips twitched. ''Paper Mite?''

Brooke's eyes narrowed. She sincerely hoped that Heather was kidding. ''Professor Breckinridge, just like before.''

Sitting down again, Heather shook her head. ''I don't know. Sounds so formal for a man who's ringing my sister's chimes.''

A warning note entered Brooke's voice. If Heather said anything to embarrass Tyler, Brooke wouldn't be able to face him. "Heather—"

"Go ahead, deny it." Heather raised her chin, challenging Brooke. "Deny that you made love with him tonight. I dare you."

Brooke clenched her teeth. "All right, I deny it."

Heather pressed her lips together in a triumphant smirk. "I don't believe you."

Dropping her head back as if in search of help that wouldn't come, Brooke moaned. "What's the use?"

Heather caught her sleeve as Brooke tried again to leave the room. "You know why I don't believe you?"

All it would take was a quick tug to free herself, but Brooke refrained, waiting. "You're going to tell me whether I ask or not."

"Because if you hadn't, you would have said so right away, instead of trying to find a way to throw me off track." Heather let go of her sister's sleeve. "You couldn't lie if your life depended on it. It's not in you."

Leaning against the stool, Brooke dragged her hand through her hair. "That's because I've had enough lies and deceptions to last a lifetime. Maybe two," she amended. "My whole life with Marc, or what I thought was my life, turned out to be a lie." She'd been such a fool then, she thought, missing all those signs that had been right in front of her if she'd only looked. "Life's too short to spend sorting out truth from fiction. I guess that's part of the reason I like Tyler. He's so straight, so honest.''

''So sexy.'' Grinning, Heather reached up and touched the reddish mark on her sister's neck. ''And probably a hell of an earth mover.'' Brooke jerked away and Heather dropped her hand.

''Don't you have work to do?'' Brooke pointed at the books spread all over the kitchen table. ''That was your excuse for not helping me with inventory tonight, remember? You said you had too much to do.''

''You should be eternally grateful to me that I bowed out tonight. Otherwise, you and the professor wouldn't have spent the evening giving new meaning to the song, 'Getting to Know You.'''

''You are impossible,'' Brooke remarked.

''Maybe,'' Heather agreed. ''But I'm happy. And I'm very proud of you, Brooke.''

At the doorway Brooke paused to look back at Heather. ''For what?''

''For getting back into the game.'' Heather raised her voice as Brooke disappeared from view. ''Remind me to send the professor a thank-you note.''

Brooke was back in the kitchen in a flash. Heather was just crazy enough to do something like that. ''You say one word to him, you even hint at one word, and you will find yourself packed up in a box of Dad's children's books and on your way to China so fast your body will be suffering from jet lag for the next decade.''

"My, my, let the woman enjoy a little sex and she turns fierce on you."

Laughing, Heather ducked, covering her head just as Brooke grabbed a dish towel and threw it at her.

Chapter Thirteen

Where did the time go?

Brooke stared at the colorful calendar beside the register as she closed the drawer after her last sale. Just yesterday, it had been Labor Day, and here they were one day away from Halloween.

The days had seemed to quickly slip by, swirling around her before they disappeared.

That was because he was in them.

Tyler.

She caught herself smiling, her reflection captured in the glass countertop. Thinking about him did that to her, made her giddy for no reason.

She made her way to the story table, where just a few minutes earlier, a group of seven kindergarteners had gathered, listening intently as she'd read a Halloween story to them. Nothing scary—she didn't believe in scary. Brooke firmly believed that childhood should be the time for believing, for laughter. Later there was time enough to learn the scarier parts. Things that had nothing to do with ghosts or goblins, but with promises not kept and dreams not realized.

Stacking the books together, she paused to take a deep breath. It was there again. That strange feeling that sneaked up on her in the midst of her happiness. A tiny kernel of uncertainty. It was as if she was waiting for a shoe to drop, a dream to end, something that would bring an abrupt rude ending to the almost idyllic existence she was enjoying.

She pressed her lips together as she began returning the books to the shelf. Things were almost too good to be true these days. That worried her. She'd learned a long time ago that when things seemed too good to be true, they usually were.

And truth meant so much to her.

Brooke sighed, shutting her eyes. She tried to put her fears out of her mind. It was the past she was reacting to, not the present. Tyler wasn't anything like Marc. Marc had come from privileged circumstances, the much-doted-on son of a fine old Boston family. Marc loved attention, Tyler seemed to shun it.

A half smile curved her mouth. She would have called Tyler shy if he hadn't been so very masculine, so in control of his surroundings.

She eased a tall thin hardcover book back amid

its brethren. The women who obviously thought Tyler attractive found no cooperation from him the way the women who had flirted with Marc had. Tyler didn't even seem to notice them. Only her.

They were so different, he and Marc.

And yet...

And yet there was something she couldn't put her finger on, something that bothered her.

Don't go there, Brooke. Don't borrow trouble, she warned herself.

Spotting a book that had been dropped under the circular table, she stooped to pick it up. The feeling wouldn't leave her.

Maybe it was because Marc had led a secret life he'd successfully kept from her for two years and Tyler's past was something he rarely talked about. Maybe that was what was weighing on her mind. When she asked Tyler questions, he always found a way to circumvent the answers.

Was that on purpose? Or just because he didn't like talking about himself?

Brooke left the book on the table. After nearly two months of sharing her soul with the man, she reluctantly had to admit that she still knew very little about him. Granted, the heart needed only a few key things to sustain its feelings, but the mind required more. Details, summations, explanations. She'd been burned once, burned badly, and maybe it was a character flaw, but she needed to know that she wasn't foolishly and blindly strolling down that same garden path again.

The silent debate went back and forth today as it did almost every day, like a furiously well-matched tennis game.

What could the man be hiding? she mocked herself. When he wasn't teaching, he was either with his girls or with her. Or both. It left precious little space to conduct a secret life.

But if that was true, if there was nothing to hide, why was he so closemouthed about his past? Why wouldn't he let her in beyond the present?

It drove her crazy.

With effort, she told herself that dwelling on it was fruitless. *Remember what happened to Pandora when she opened that damn box, which could have just as easily remained closed? If it had, both she and the world would have suffered the less for it.*

But that was a fairy tale, a myth, and this was life she was dealing with. Her life.

Would she suffer if she pushed a little harder, delved a little further into his past? She didn't know. The truth didn't always set you free. Sometimes it trapped you into following a course you would have otherwise avoided. A course that led only to despair.

"Hi." Entering the store, Heather deposited her backpack behind the counter. Startled, Brooke jerked up her head. "My God, you look as if you've just discovered the Internet was going to be giving away free children's books from now until the end of the year." Heather peered at her face. "Are you all right?"

Embarrassed, Brooke pretended to be busy with

shuffling the books on display next to the register. "Just thinking."

"Good thinking or bad thinking?" Heather asked.

Brooke hesitated, debating how much to say. "Wondering."

Shrugging out of her sweater, Heather tossed it on top of her backpack. It was one of her shorter days, and she'd decided to help Brooke out for a couple of hours before the store closed. "About?"

"Tyler."

Heather laughed. "No-brainer there. Terrific catch for someone like you."

Brooke stopped rearranging the books. "What do you mean, someone like me?"

Heather grinned. She knew that would get her.

"He's sexy but safe, obviously a family man. Brilliant." Heather was only repeating what she'd heard said over quickly grabbed lunches in the Studio Arts Department cafeteria. She'd made it a point to hang around there several times to see if she could pick up any information about the man who was figuring so prominently in her sister's life these days.

Brooke fisted a hand on her hip. She knew Heather had stopped seeing Simon. "And by contrast, you like dull, dangerous loners who are stupid, right?"

Heather shook her head. "The key phrase here is 'family man.' I, for one, am not looking to get tied down."

Brooke sniffed and attempted to sound indifferent. "Neither am I."

"Ha!" If ever there was a homebody, it was Brooke. Heather's laugh faded. They were alone in the store for the moment. Both knew how temporary that could be, but she seized the opportunity, anyway. Heather slipped her arm around Brooke. "Seriously, what's the problem?"

There was no use pretending that nothing was bothering her. Heather could see right through her. "The problem is, I don't really know very much about him," Brooke replied.

Odd, Heather thought. Brooke could usually get a statue to open up. She had the same way about her that their father'd had. Still, that didn't seem like much of a problem. "So, ask."

"I did," Brooke confessed. Heather raised a brow. "The man can do an incredible verbal sashay. He hardly answers anything."

Knowing minute details had never been very important to Heather, but she could see why it might spook Brooke, given her past. Heather tried to make light of it. "And you're afraid he's secretly a serial killer?"

"I'm afraid that secretly he might be Marc."

"No way," Heather dismissed the idea. Brooke looked unconvinced. "But there are ways to find things out, you know."

"I'm not going to spy on him."

"Not spy, just peek a little," Heather replied.

"No." What if Tyler found out somehow?

Brooke wondered. What would he think? For that matter, how would *she* feel if she discovered that he was looking into her background? No, anything she learned about Tyler's past would have to come from him.

Heather shrugged. "Suit yourself."

"I will." Rounding the counter, Brooke crossed to a display. "Just as soon as I find out what that is," she murmured under her breath.

She was being paranoid. Tyler was a wonderful man and she was lucky he had happened into her life. So what if he wasn't vocal about his past? It was probably because the past hurt too much. Everyone had a fault, and his was being secretive. There were far worse things he could be. And given time, she believed he would open up to her. She just had to be patient.

Brooke tried to tell herself that she was preaching to the choir, but deep down, she was afraid that maybe it was actually more like the line from Macbeth about the lady protesting too much.

Brooke smiled to herself. The only thing that rushed was her blood whenever she was around him.

"I really appreciate this, Brooke," Tyler said.

On her knees, Brooke was busy adjusting Stephany's wings. The other two angels, otherwise known as Bethany and Tiffany, waited their turns. She was taking them trick-or-treating while Tyler, swamped with work, was going to remain behind to answer the door and hand out treats, and possibly get a little work done in between.

Beside Brooke on the living-room coffee table was a huge platter of Oma's sugar cookies in various Halloween shapes, while the biggest bowl she had ever seen stood next to it, filled to the brim with at least ten different kinds of individually wrapped candy. She figured Tyler had to have put a real dent in the local supermarket's supply.

"The pleasure is all mine." She gave him a smile over her shoulder, then turned to Tiffany. "I love trick-or-treating. Taking the girls around gives me an excuse to play out my fantasy."

Not completely to his surprise, she'd come dressed in a costume. A genie that rivaled any gut-tightening adolescent fantasy he might have had. It brought new meaning to the phrase *trick-or-treat* for him.

Finished, Brooke rose to her feet. On his way to fetch his camera to immortalize the girls' first Halloween in Bedford, he paused to give Brooke an unabashed leer, turning so that the girls didn't see.

"Come back in that costume," he whispered, "and it might give me a chance to act out one of my old fantasies."

"You've got yourself a deal." She winked, wishing it could be more than just empty talk. But she knew that he'd never think of doing anything in the same house where his daughters slept. It was laudable, even though it was frustrating at the same time.

"Aren't we pretty, Daddy?" Tiffany spun around,

a swirl of pink nylon and tulle. Her sisters, Stephany in blue and Bethany in yellow, immediately followed suit. They looked like three animated pinwheels.

He pretended to cover his eyes. "I don't know if I can take so much gorgeousness."

"Gorgeousness? Well, it's a cinch you couldn't get work as an English teacher," Brooke quipped.

He gave her a look. "I'll deal with you later."

She sighed. "Promises, promises."

"Don't anyone move," Tyler warned. "I'll be right back." He strode quickly to the stairs. If he remembered correctly, the last time he'd seen the camera it was in his bedroom closet.

Tyler was halfway up when the telephone rang.

Automatically looking at his watch, he silently swore.

With all the excitement going on, he'd forgotten that it was time for his sister's weekly call.

Turning, he flew down the stairs. Just in time to see Brooke replacing the receiver.

Damn.

He tried to read the expression on her face, but it told him nothing. He nodded at the telephone. "Who was that just now?"

"Wrong number." Unable to resist, Brooke took a candy from the bowl. "Some woman asking for someone named Tom. I guess she must have realized she'd misdialed. She hung up before I could tell her there was no one here by that name."

Balling up the empty wrapper, Brooke looked

around for somewhere to throw it away. Out of the corner of her eye she saw the look on Tyler's face. He looked vaguely annoyed with himself. The next minute the expression was gone.

"Were you expecting a call?"

The question sounded innocent enough. Did she suspect anything? he wondered. "No, why?"

She shrugged again, the costume sliding off her shoulder. Brooke tugged it back into place. "You seem a little, I don't know, anticipatory? As if you were waiting for something."

Avoiding her eyes, Tyler looked, instead, at his daughters. "Yes, for the trick-or-treaters to launch their attack." Tyler indicated the window. "Well, it's dark. Maybe you should get started."

Was he trying to get her to leave? An uneasiness she'd thought had finally left made a fleeting reappearance. "Didn't you want to take a photograph of the girls?"

Preoccupied, he didn't hear her. He glanced up. "What?"

"A photograph." Brooke spread out her hands, indicating the triplets. "You were going upstairs to get your camera, remember?"

He tried not to look at his watch, knowing it would look conspicuous. Carla was going to call again at any moment. But maybe he still had time to get the camera. "Oh, right, sure. Just hold it a minute." He froze as the phone rang again, his mind scrambling for a solution. "Um, maybe you'd better go.'' He kissed three upturned mouths quickly. ''I'll take a photograph when you get back.''

Brooke nodded at the telephone. ''Want me to get that?'' she asked.

''No!'' Annoyed with himself, he lowered his voice. ''I'll pick it up in the study. One of the other professors said he'd call.''

But he'd just said that he wasn't expecting a call. She stared after him for a minute, puzzled. Why didn't he just answer it here first, then put it on hold, instead of hurrying to the den?

''Let's go!'' Tiffany begged, tugging on Brooke's arm. ''Halloween's gonna be over before we go out.''

''Not unless we walk very very slowly,'' Brooke assured her. Unable to resist the temptation, Brooke glanced down at the telephone on the coffee table. Tyler had caller ID, presumably to screen unwanted calls.

The number on the screen was preceded by an out-of-state area code—212. New York, she remembered. Just like the earlier wrong number. Exactly like the earlier wrong number, Brooke realized as the phone number played across the screen of her mind.

But if it was a wrong number, why did the light remain on? Was he talking to the woman, instead of hanging up? Why, if he didn't know her?

Or did he?

If a woman answers, hang up. Wasn't that the credo of the ''other woman''?

Questions and half-formed thoughts began breeding, racing through her mind.

When they'd first met, Tyler had told her he'd never been to New York. So who was calling? Who was Tom, and why had the woman hung up when she'd heard Brooke's voice?

Uneasiness began to knit together inside her. "Brooke, please, can't we go?" Stephany asked shyly.

The entreaty broke through her thoughts. Brooke forced a smile to her lips. "Okay, angels, let's get this show on the road."

Stephany looked at Bethany. "'Spression?"

"'Spression," the girl assured her wisely.

Brooke could have eaten them all up then and there. She tried to concentrate on her affection for the girls and not the suspicions forming about their father.

It was a public telephone. The person who had called Tyler last night had called from a public telephone.

Brooke had struggled with her conscience all night, long after she'd brought the girls home, long after she had gone home herself, turning down Tyler's offer of a nightcap.

The following morning, with perhaps two hours of disjointed sleep to her credit, Brooke had nervously tapped out the numbers she remembered, afraid of what or who she would find on the other end.

But the phone rang and rang without an answer. She tried several times, all in succession. Finally, a gruff voice had answered and cursed her roundly, demanding to know what she was doing, calling a pay phone on the corner of Sixth Avenue and Fiftieth Street. Apparently he was. a pushcart vendor and she was annoying his transient clientele.

She'd hung up, feeling unsettled, with even more questions than before. Who'd called Tyler from a city he claimed never to have set foot in?

Admittedly there might have been a dozen reasons the call could have come from there. But none that made sense to her. Not at that time of night. Not from a public phone located in the middle of Manhattan.

What was going on?

And how could she find out without asking? Without making it seem as if she was spying on him? Because that was what it was, she thought, listlessly stirring her coffee, which had grown cold. Spying. If the tables had been turned, she wouldn't have appreciated him doing this to her.

But the tables couldn't have been turned, she thought. She would have told him anything he wanted to know.

Then why haven't you told him about Marc?

She was going to. She made up her mind. First chance she got. The subject hadn't come up, but that was no excuse.

Trust. It came down to a matter of trust, she thought. She was just going to have to trust him.

But how could she trust him if he didn't trust her enough to tell her anything?

Brooke passed her hand over her brow. She was working her way into one whopper of a headache.

Tyler wanted to see her again. That, and he felt a little uneasy about last night. She'd looked at him so oddly just before she took the girls out. Just after the telephone call had come in. He wanted to make it up to her.

So he'd asked Brooke out to dinner to the restaurant where they had gone that first time. Heather had offered to stay with the girls. They were almost as crazy about her as they were about Brooke. As he was about Brooke.

He knew he was living in a fool's paradise, but even fools had the right to be happy for a little while.

Brooke had seemed preoccupied all through dinner. He wondered if it had to do with last night and fervently hoped it didn't.

"A penny for your thoughts," he murmured.

She was still struggling with questions and trying not to. Looking up, she smiled and said evasively, "I'm too tired to have thoughts."

Tilting his head to one side, he looked at her more closely. "Now that you mention it, you do look as if you're drooping a little. Why didn't you say something? We could have gone out another night."

How many nights did they have left together? One? Five? Fifty? She clutched at the first excuse that occurred to her. "Maybe I ate too much. Too much food always makes me feel sleepy."

The band had just begun playing. Something snappy would have been better, but this would do. "I have the prefect remedy for that."

"What?" she asked as he got to his feet, taking her hand.

"Dance with me." He drew her to her feet. "You can't sleep if you're moving."

His hand joined with hers, Tyler led her out onto the floor.

She was being silly, she thought as he took her into his arms, having doubts about him. She'd never been happier in her whole life. Happier or more secure. She was just going to have to stop seeing threats where none existed.

Sighing softly, she laid her head against his shoulder and let the slow music drift into her being as her body melded into his.

She felt him press a kiss to the top of her head. Her eyes fluttered shut in utter contentment. "You know, if you're tired, I can take you home. I love being with you, but I don't want to be selfish about this."

"That's okay. I'm due for my second wind." Straightening, she blinked her eyes, then opened them wide. "See, here it is, ready to take hold. I'm awake now."

Laughing, he inclined his head and brushed his lips over hers.

The next moment someone was tapping Tyler on

the shoulder. He looked up reluctantly. Then silently swore.

"It *is* you. I looked across the floor and nearly fainted dead away. Tom. Tom Conway. This is so exciting for me."

Startled, Brooke jerked her head away only to look into the face of a tall thin woman who was pressing her hand to her slight breast as her eyes all but devoured Tyler.

Chapter Fourteen

The stranger's fingers were on Tyler's arm, lightly grasping his sleeve. There was an embarrassed-looking older man with thinning brown hair standing a few feet behind the woman, silently observing what was happening.

"I was such a fan," the woman gushed. "*Am* such a fan," she corrected with a nervous laugh. "I still have my program from that concert you gave in Philadelphia. Why did you ever stop performing?" The question was half-reproachful, ending in a whine.

Everything froze inside Tyler. All along he'd been worried about something like this happening. But nothing had really prepared him. And just now his mind had been elsewhere. On the woman in his arms.

With steely control, he managed not to allow his expression to change. Instead, he looked the erstwhile fan in the eyes and lied.

"I'm afraid you've gotten me confused with someone else, madam." He'd gotten good at lies. For the most part they had become his constant companion until even he had difficulty in sorting out the lies from the truth. It wasn't anything he was proud of.

The woman looked flustered and then determined. Convinced she wasn't mistaken, she shook her head adamantly.

"That's not possible. I saw you. I had a perfect seat right in front. It cost me an entire week's pay. Third row, center. And your picture was in the program. It's you. I know it's you." She fixed her watery brown eyes on him as if that would make him confess. "You're Tom Conway."

Tyler had no idea where the calmness came from, but it was suddenly there, flowing through him. He heard himself laugh. It was a kind tolerant sound. "I assure you, I am not now, nor have I ever been this Tom Conway." He paused as if trying to place the name. "Who is he—some rock star?"

"No, no, he's a pianist," the woman replied. Her confusion was obvious. Then, as if she was required to champion the man she'd thought him to be, the woman lifted her head and looked Tyler directly in the eye. "Just about the greatest pianist I've ever heard. You—he," she corrected herself uncertainly, her eyes moving back and forth quickly as if to peel away any mask that might be in place, "disappeared several years ago. Stopped giving concerts," she said. "And when I saw you here…" Her voice, now deflated, trailed away. The uncertainty grew. "I'm sorry."

He could afford to be gracious. It hid his true feelings. "No harm done."

Apparently crestfallen, the woman paused before finally turning back to her partner. "He looks just like him," she muttered.

"I could have told you Conway was taller if you'd asked." The man's voice had a superior air as he ushered her away.

Giving no sign that he'd just been a man on the brink of being unmasked, Tyler resumed dancing with Brooke. "I guess it's true what they say."

Feeling vaguely disturbed, Brooke glanced over her shoulder at the woman. But she had already disappeared into the background shadows. "What?"

"Everyone's got a double somewhere." He wanted to avoid her eyes, but knew that was a mistake. So he kept his smile carefully in place. An amused tolerant one. "This Tom Conway obviously must be mine. I wonder if he's as good as she thinks he is." He laughed softly. "Probably not."

A double.

What he was saying was perfectly plausible, but it still bothered Brooke. A lot of things were beginning to bother her, rubbing against her thoughts like tiny, tiny rocks imbedded in her shoe. She chewed on her lower lip, wondering if she should refrain from saying anything.

But she couldn't. "What an odd coincidence."

"What is?" Tyler asked.

She looked up at him. "That woman who called last night. She was looking for a Tom, too."

Moving her to the side as another couple came a bit too close, he shrugged carelessly. "Tom's a common enough name."

"I suppose."

She sounded completely unconvinced. God, but he didn't want her going there. Not yet. He didn't want this to end yet. He knew they had no future together, but still... He had never believed that he could possibly care about anyone else. Now that he'd found he could and did, he was reluctant to let it end so abruptly.

"There is another explanation, you know."

Open to suggestion, she looked up at him. He seemed to fill up all the space around them. Just the way he was filling up her world. She told herself she was ridiculous to harbor suspicions about this man. He looked so open and honest.

"And that is?"

He lowered his lids, giving himself a vaguely sinister look. "That I'm actually an international jewel thief who poses as different people in different parts of the world."

Brooke laughed at the absurd notion. It *was* silly to be suspicious. "All the while carting around three little girls in your wake," she remarked.

"Ah, but they're not little girls." With a wink he drew her closer to him. "They're really my thirty-four-year-old accomplices. Couldn't pull off jewel heists without them."

Laughing, she surrendered. "All right, all right, you've proved your point."

"Good." Resting his cheek against her hair, Tyler closed his eyes and slowly let out the breath he'd been holding. That had been close. Too close.

He fervently hoped that earned him a respite.

They left soon afterward. Not wanting to tempt fate or flaunt his presence near the tall thin woman, whom he'd noticed glancing at him several times that evening, Tyler told Brooke that he had an early meeting with the department head before classes began.

Edgy, she unlocked her front door and turned to look at him. She didn't want the evening to end. "I guess that means you don't feel like stopping in for a few minutes."

Temptation was beginning to weave a web around him. He struggled with it. "No, it means I can't stop in." His eyes met hers. "But that doesn't mean I don't want to."

"Oh." A confident smile began to emerge on her lips. "I see."

Raising herself slightly on her toes, she wove her arms around his neck. And kissed him hard on the mouth. Hard and with enough feeling to completely detonate his inner workings in one wild burst.

The kiss deepened and he leaned his body into hers, hooking one arm around her waist to pull her closer. Her confidence grew. Brooke felt behind her for the doorknob. Turning it, she pushed the door open softly. Just as she did, she drew her lips a fraction of an inch away. Just enough to make him move forward.

Reluctant to break contact, Tyler found himself moving with her. And then smiling against her mouth when he realized that he had somehow managed to get halfway into the foyer.

The smile crinkled up to his eyes as they found hers. "Well, if you put it that way."

Brooke took another step back, her face the picture of innocence. "What way?"

"A way I just can't resist." Closing the door behind him without bothering to look, he slipped his arms around her waist and pulled her to him again. "Why is it that the more I make love with you, the more I want to?"

He was giving voice to the exact same thoughts she had. "Some things are just habit-forming, I guess," Brooke said.

When she felt his hands dip lower, molding her hips to his, Brooke had to concentrate to keep her eyes from fluttering shut. An invisible switch seemed to go off somewhere. Her body began heating.

Anticipation moved forward for a front-row seat.

"I guess," he echoed, cupping her cheek with his hand. The softness of her skin made him ache to touch her all over. "A habit. Too bad I don't seem to have the energy to break it."

That was the last thing she wanted—him to walk away. Not after she'd finally found someone so special. Someone who made her feel so special. "Don't even think about it."

Amused, he inclined his head obediently. "Your wish is my command."

The truth was, he was trying very hard not to think about it. About the grip this had on him. Because if he thought about it, then he would have to think about how unfair all this was to her.

Forced to live within a house constructed of lies, he still didn't like it. Didn't like that he couldn't share himself with her in the true meaning of the word. All he could do was give her physical evidence of the way he felt.

But what counted, the man he really was, he wasn't free to reveal.

And when she discovered this deception, whether now or later, she wouldn't be able to forgive him. He knew her. Knew her better than she probably knew herself.

But if he was lucky, that day wouldn't come for a very long while.

Brooke forced air into her lungs. He was making her crazy, cupping her breasts, moving his palms over them. Dressed, she felt as if she was completely naked. Ached to be completely naked. "I thought you said you had an early day tomorrow."

Finding the zipper in back of her dress, he slid it

down, pressing his lips to her neck. He felt her pulse jump. His loins tightened. "I do."

She was having trouble forming sentences. "Don't you want to go to bed?"

"I'm working on it." He slipped the dress down her arms. It sank to the floor. She was wearing stockings. Not panty hose, stockings. He wanted to take her this instant. "As fast as I can."

"No, I meant home." She stepped out of her shoes, instantly becoming three inches shorter. "To your bed."

Kissing first one shoulder, then the other, he coaxed the straps of her bra down to half-mast. "Not particularly."

Excitement churned her stomach. She dug her fingers into his arms as she felt the bra clasp give at her back. "If you stay, you won't get much sleep."

Hands on the sides of her breasts, he eased the straps along the swell, drawing away the fabric as he moved. He was making both of them crazy. "I've gone without sleep before."

Her knees were beginning to give. "You'll be exhausted in the morning."

He left her wearing only lacy white underwear and flesh-colored stockings that teased her thighs and his resistance. He nipped her lower lip, drawing it between his own before releasing it. "Some things are worth the price."

A laugh bubbled up from her throat, rumbling against his lips. But then she placed her hands over his, stopping him. When he raised his eyes to her face, he saw she was serious. Dread twisted in his gut.

This was moving far more swiftly than she'd ever thought it would. He'd all but swept her off her feet, he and his daughters. She knew that she was falling in love with him. Knew all the signs of the condition and knew she had a terminal case of it. But before she sank any deeper into it, she needed him to know something. It was only fair.

"We have to talk," she said.

The words mocked him, threatening to destroy the foundationless castle he'd sought shelter in. He strove to hold on a little longer. He moved his hands to her buttocks, kneading them. He saw desire flare in her eyes. "We can do that later," he said, "when I'm too tired to make a move on you."

Though it was hard, she moved his hands back to her waist. She was determined to do this now, before her courage faltered. "No, really."

Relenting, he waited. This was about the incident in the restaurant. She was going to ask questions. Questions he'd been forbidden to answer. He braced himself. "What's wrong?"

She hunted for the right words. When they didn't come, she used ones that were available, stumbling through it. "I need to tell you something. It's not a big deal, really. I mean, this kind of thing goes on all the time, and maybe I'm making too much of it, but—"

Dammit, she was rambling. Taking a breath, she

wondered how he was going to take this. Wondered if it would matter to him.

Please don't let it matter to him.

Because it had stopped mattering to her.

"I was married."

"Was," he repeated. Was that it? A confession? He didn't know whether to feel relieved or incredibly guilty. "As in past tense?"

She nodded. "As in past tense. I've been divorced for two years." She caught her lower lip between her teeth. "I don't know why I didn't tell you sooner. It's just not something I share with people." She searched his face. "It doesn't make a difference, does it?"

Despite the inappropriateness, he felt like singing. This wasn't about him. She wasn't backing away.

"No." Framing her face in his hands, he kissed her quickly, then drew his head back. "Should it?"

Her relief was tremendous. She tried to pull her thoughts together. She wanted him to understand just what a giant step she'd taken. And what he meant to her.

"Well, it did to me. When I got divorced, I swore I'd never get married again." Did he understand what she was saying? How grateful she was to him for waking up all these feelings inside her? For making her realize she could feel something again beyond betrayal? "Until you came along, I was pretty much of a hermit."

He nodded solemnly. His lips twitched at the end,

giving him away. "I could tell by the barbwire-barricaded one-room shack."

She swatted at him, the laughter back in her eyes. "I meant emotionally."

He wanted to devour her right then and there, but he held himself in check. This confession meant a great deal to her. "So what happened? Irreconcilable differences?" He saw her eyes harden for just a moment.

"In a way, yes. He was a pathological liar and I was pathologically hooked on the truth." She sighed, shaking her head. It all seemed so long ago now. "I met him in college. He was studying to become a doctor." Her smile was disparaging. "Little did I realize it was because his lifelong dream was to play doctor every chance he got with every beautiful female who crossed his path. I was just too stupid to realize what was going on until I walked in on him one day." Even now the memory hurt. Hurt because she'd given her heart to someone who didn't deserve it. Hurt because when she had needed him most was when she'd discovered that she was in love with a stranger. "It was just after my father had died. I flew back early from the funeral and found Marc in bed with his lab technician."

Combing his hands through her hair, he framed her face. "Brooke, I'm sorry."

She knew he was and her heart quickened. "These things happen."

That was what her lawyer had said to her. However, these "things" might happen to other people, but she'd never dreamed they would happen to her.

Free of the burden at last, wanting to put it all behind her, Brooke raised her gaze to his. "Make love with me, Tyler. Now. Please."

He put his finger to her lips, silencing them. "Shh. You don't have to ask for something I've been dying to do all evening. Do you have any idea how hard it is to dance with you, to hold you in my arms on a crowded floor when all I want to do is—"

It was her turn to silence him. Spreading her fingers along his mouth, she fell in love with him for the first time. All over again.

"Don't talk. Show me."

He did.

Feverishly.

The gentleness was still there, but a little less so, perhaps because his desire was more intense. Because he was reacting to her words, to her needs and to the sobering fact that this relationship had nearly ended tonight. If that woman had been a little more forceful or Brooke had been a little more suspicious, things might have blown up in his face.

If not right there, then soon afterward.

He didn't know how much longer he could continue lying to her. And yet he couldn't tell her the truth. If she came to him now demanding it, he couldn't tell her. Not because he'd sworn an oath or given his word, though he had, but because there were other lives than just his own involved. Lives he'd gladly give up his own for.

So he took her in the foyer, without bothering to venture any farther into the house, without leaving the small area that confined them. His needs wouldn't wait that long.

He was quick tonight. Quicker than she could ever remember him being. But then, she'd never asked him to make love with her before. Maybe that inspired him. His reaction certainly inspired her. She couldn't wait to tear his clothes from his body, though she took care at the end not to rip anything. One of the triplets would be keen-eyed enough to notice. She didn't want him beset with questions he couldn't answer.

So she tried to steady her hands as she pulled his shirt out of his pants, tried to be careful as her fingers undid the buttons in rapid succession. Tried hard not to irreparably yank apart the zipper to his trousers.

He could feel the frenzy that seemed to take possession of her. Could taste it on her mouth, smell it on her body. It nearly drove him insane. What would he do if she walked away from him?

If?

The word was *when*, not *if*.

But that was a time he couldn't allow himself to think about now. That was for later. Later would come, heavy with consequences and penalties. But he had now, and now all he wanted was to lose himself in her, to give her what she wanted and thereby fulfill himself. Because she was his beginning and his ending, and he wanted nothing more than to be with her, always.

Even while he knew that *always* was, for him, a sadly finite word.

And then she was nude before him. Nude, making his blood rush, his loins pulse and his thoughts burn up in the heat of his desire. Tyler ran his hands over her, as if to assure himself that she was still here. Still, for now, his.

Caressing every curve, sealing his mouth to hers, he brought her to the floor with him. A heap of clothing, his and hers, cushioned her body from the hard tile.

Gasping, trying hard not to cry out, she withered against the rumpled clothing as his lips left hers and anointed, with slow deliberate open-mouth kisses, the rest of her body.

She was damp and growing damper. Sharp spears of sweet anguish shot through her as she felt his lips, tongue and teeth travel the length of her. Pausing to suckle here, to tease there. Making her belly quiver as he encircled her navel before moving lower. The dampness increased, fueled by anticipation.

When she felt the thrust of his tongue, her fingers dug in, finding nothing to clutch. One of her nails broke against the tile as she arched against his mouth, trying desperately to absorb the sensation he created as it exploded through her core.

Slick sweat covered her as she fell back. A moment later, her heart hammering wildly in her breast, she saw his eyes above hers, his body poised.

Very slowly, holding her gaze, Tyler slipped inside her. Made them one.

With the last of her energy, she tightened around him and began to move. Faster and faster until they both found what they were looking for. And fell to earth together in a single exhausted sigh.

Tyler held her for a long time, listening to her breathe. Praying for just a little more time.

Chapter Fifteen

Heather stared moodily at the textbook in front of her, not seeing a single word. Some child psychologist she was going to make. She couldn't even find her way out of her own dilemma.

Closing her eyes, she tilted the chair back on two legs and rocked, thinking. The right thing to do was to tell Brooke exactly what she'd discovered. But the right thing wasn't always the right thing.

She sighed, wishing she'd never followed her impulse. Now it was too late. She knew too much.

"You know, Heather, you've been moping around the house for two days."

Jolted back into her surroundings, Heather's eyes flew open as her chair came crashing back down to all fours. Brooke had somehow managed to come home without her hearing and was now standing in front of her, frowning.

"If you miss Simon, why don't you call him?"

"Simon?" Heather blinked, confused. "What makes you think I miss Simon?"

Hungry, Brooke went to the refrigerator and began looking for sandwich fixings. Anything fancier would require more energy than she had at her disposal at the moment.

"Simple. You've been roaming around, acting like a wounded bear for the last few days." She tossed a head of lettuce on the counter, followed by a loaf of bread and a package of cold cuts. "If it isn't Simon, then what is bothering you?"

For a second Heather entertained the idea of going with the excuse that Brooke offered her, but that would be lying. She knew how Brooke felt about lying. Which was what made this so damn hard to tell her.

But it had to be told.

Heather took a deep breath and saw Brooke look at her oddly.

"This isn't about me and Simon. It's…" Heather licked her lips, feeling uncustomarily shaky. She hated doing this to Brooke, but if she didn't, who knew how hurt her sister could get? "It's about you and Tyler. Or whoever he is."

About to reach for the jar of mayonnaise, Brooke stopped. "Me and Tyler?"

"Or whoever he is," Heather repeated.

"Why are you saying that?"

Heather hated this, but in all good conscience, she couldn't keep quiet about it, either. They needed to get to the bottom of this mystery. For Brooke's sake. "Because there's no record of Tyler Breckinridge beyond the last four months. No driver's license..."

Was that all? Relieved, Brooke laughed it off. "He moved here from another state."

Heather knew what Brooke was trying to do, and her heart ached for her sister. But since she'd started, there was no turning back. "Did he also move here from outer space?"

Half angry, half frightened, Brooke glared at her sister. "What are you talking about?"

Heather twisted around in her chair to face Brooke. "He has no tax records. There are no income-tax forms filed under his name."

"How did you find out something like that?"

Heather's shrug was exasperated, dismissive. "I have friends."

"What kind of friends?" Brooke asked incredulously. "Ex-CIA agents?"

"No."

What was Heather trying to do? Why was she saying this? "Current CIA agents?" Brooke demanded, only half joking.

Heather got to her feet and dragged her hand through her hair. Frustrated for her sister, for herself. And angry as hell at the man who was putting them both through this, whatever his reasons. "I talked to some friends who know how to surf the web for sensitive material, but my friends are not the issue here. You're not focusing, Brooke."

"Maybe I don't want to," she whispered. Brooke shut her eyes. This couldn't be happening. Not again. The man she was in love with couldn't be lying to her so blatantly. There had to be some mistake. She struggled to find it. "Information gets messed up all the time, Heather. You know that." A panicky desperation had her searching for supporting facts. Without realizing it, she began pacing.

"The letter that gets lost for forty years," Brooke said, "then turns up in someone's mailbox. The credit histories that destroy a person's life wind up being due to a typo. The IRS sending ordinary citizens letters saying they owe back taxes equal to their social-security numbers—these are all glitches, usually because of some computer malfunction." Suddenly aware that she was roaming the length of the kitchen, she turned back to Heather. "For some reason, Tyler's information got folded, spindled or mutilated somehow. No big thing."

Heather's heart went out to Brooke. "If you say so."

Brooke took the words for what they were, doled-out sympathy. Anger washed over her. "Who told you you had the right to play detective, anyway?"

Heather felt better with Brooke shouting at her. Then she didn't have to dwell on how guilty she felt for being the one to tell her. "*I* told me. Because I care about you, Brooke, and you had these questions and I just didn't want to see you hurt again by some guy.''

Brooke's laugh was short, hollow. ''So you elected to take on the job yourself?''

Heather shoved her hands in her pockets, helpless. The last thing in the world she wanted to do was hurt Brooke. ''Hey, look, I didn't mean...''

Getting angry at Heather wasn't going to solve anything. It wasn't Heather's fault these discrepancies existed. Brooke felt moisture gathering in her eyes. She wasn't going to cry. She wasn't.

She waved Heather into silence. ''That's okay.'' Her voice felt hollow. As hollow as her heart. ''Just leave me alone for a while, all right? I've got some thinking to do.'' Brooke sank into the kitchen chair as if she was a puppet and all her strings had suddenly been cut and there was nothing holding her up any longer.

Heather quickly gathered up her books from the table. She slanted a concerned look at Brooke's face. ''Are you going to be all right?''

''Probably not.'' Brooke lifted her head and forced a thin smile. ''But I will be eventually.'' The thin smile turned contrite. ''I didn't mean to yell at you.''

''Forget it.'' Books pressed to her chest, Heather stopped in the doorway for a second before going upstairs. ''At least you didn't kill the messenger.''

Brooke dropped her head into her hands. She wasn't going to think about it, wasn't going to let herself get carried away or excited, not until she had a chance to talk to Tyler. Not until she gave *him* a chance to explain this all away.

The phone call with the New York area code came back to haunt her, anyway. The phone call and the woman from the other night who'd been so adamant about Tyler being this Tom Conway person.

Was there a Tom Conway? Was that who Tyler really was? Why would he change his name?

She didn't want to find out if she was right. Didn't want to discover that she had been lied to by a man she was beginning to care about very much. To love. But she couldn't close her eyes to it. That would make her a party to lying to herself.

Brooke sat in the kitchen for a very long time, struggling with her conscience, with her fears. Finally, when she couldn't take it any longer, she went into the den and turned on the computer. She had a few resources of her own to access. With any luck, they would smother her fears and put them to rest.

"Are you Tom Conway?"

Startled Tyler looked up from the papers he was grading in the small office the music department had allotted him. He'd been trying to decide whether to be lenient or the kind of demanding teacher who forced his students to live up to their potential. Brooke was standing in the doorway, her face pale.

A feeling of dread suddenly pushed forward. "What did you say?"

Brooke closed the door at her back, her eyes never

leaving his face. Daring him to lie to her. "Are you Tom Conway?"

The quiet undemanding voice sliced the air like a well-honed saber. He tried to find a way to answer without answering. "Brooke, that woman was a nearsighted fan who saw dark hair, a tall frame and let her imagination take it from there."

He hadn't answered her question. Her fears were gelling. She pushed the envelope further. "So you know what this Tom Conway looks like?"

He shrugged helplessly. "I'm making assumptions—" Dammit, why did this have to happen now? He'd been wrestling with his conscience all along, searching for a way out of this. But he needed more time to come up with something everyone could live with.

And now there wasn't any more time.

"I made a few assumptions, too." Her voice was devoid of emotion. It was as if she was burned out inside. "But now I realize that I'm still, despite everything, too trusting. Not at first, but because I wanted to believe that someone I was growing to care about wouldn't tell me bald-faced lies."

He saw the hurt in her eyes. It drove a shaft through him. "Brooke—"

She didn't stop, couldn't stop, because if she did, she was going to break down. This hurt more than she'd thought possible. So much more than discovering that Marc had been cheating on her.

Her hands on the back of the chair for support,

she tried very hard to sound detached. She couldn't quite pull it off.

"I did a little Internet surfing last night. Do you know that with enough time, patience and search engines, you can come up with almost anything? Find the most obscure facts. There's even a Web site that auctions off out-of-print, hard-to-find record albums." She struggled to keep the tears out of her voice. "Tom Conway should be very flattered. His albums are pulling in some pretty fair bids." She drew back when she saw Tyler reach out to her. "They even had a reproduction of one of the album covers. And the funny thing is, that woman was right. You do look a lot like him." There was no way she could keep the bitterness from surfacing in her voice. The shock had been overwhelming. "Actually, more like his older brother, but that could be because the album was more than fifteen years old."

Like a drowning man trying desperately to hold on to a branch to keep himself afloat a moment longer, he continued to look for a way out. "What does all this have to do with me?"

"That's what I'd like to know." She leaned over the desk. "I want you to look me in the eye. In the eye, dammit," she repeated. He raised his eyes to hers. "And tell me you're not Tom Conway." When he hesitated, she had her answer. Brooke straightened. "That's what I thought." Everything inside her was trembling, whether with rage or despair, she didn't know. "Would you mind telling me why?"

"Why?" he echoed, looking at her blankly.

"Don't act dumb. It doesn't become you no matter what your name is." It was all she could do to keep from shouting at him. She was aware that people were passing the small partially glass-enclosed office and looking in curiously. "Why did you lie to everyone about who you were?" With a feverish desperation, she sought an absolving explanation. "Are you in some sort of trouble? Just tell me what's going on and I'll help. But I can't help if you won't trust me."

With all his heart, he wished he could tell her everything. But he had been instructed. Warned. "Brooke, I can't."

"I see." It was over. Utterly over. She was standing in the middle of ashes, and she hadn't the good sense to back away. She blew out a breath. "Maybe this doesn't really matter to you, but it took an awful lot for me to trust you. To get over my fear of being played for a fool—"

"I didn't play you for a fool—"

How could he possibly say that? "You lied to me, *are* lying to me. That's being played for a fool in my book."

Tyler leapt to his feet, rounded the desk and caught her by the arms, holding her in place. He didn't know what else to do. "Look, Brooke, this isn't my choice—"

Shaking him off, she stepped back. Her eyes warned him not to try that again.

"Isn't it? The bottom line is that we all make our own choices, no matter what anyone else says.

That's what makes us individuals. Now you can either choose to trust me or choose not to. If not, then I'm sorry, but I can't see you anymore. I can't have someone in my life who doesn't trust me enough to tell me the truth." She drew herself up. She felt for the doorknob behind her and turned it. "Goodbye, Tyler, or Tom, or whoever you are."

It couldn't end this way, Tyler thought. "Brooke, wait," he called.

But she didn't.

To Heather, this was far worse than anything that had gone on after Brooke had returned home and told her she was getting a divorce. Then there had been anger and hot words. Now it was as if Brooke had vanished into some sort of netherworld and all that was left behind was this shell of a woman who went through the motions of living.

It was like living with a zombie. Heather couldn't take seeing Brooke this way anymore. "You know, if you don't call him, I will."

Brooke slanted a look at her sister as the latter walked to the coffee table, her hand outstretched. "Touch that telephone and you're a dead woman."

Deciding it was better not to test that, Heather stopped. "Brooke, you can't go on this way."

"I won't." Brooke looked down at the book in her lap. The one she'd been staring at for the past twenty minutes without absorbing a single word. The lines swam in front of her. "I'll get over it. But right now, I'm wallowing, and I'll thank you to leave and let me wallow in peace.''

Torn, Heather took a step toward the hall and then stopped. "Brooke, you've been like this for almost two weeks."

"And I'll be like this for however long it takes me to get over the mystery man." Annoyed, frustrated, Brooke gave in to her impulse and threw the book she wasn't reading against the wall.

"Feel better?" Heather asked, looking at the book lying on the floor.

Brooke got to her feet, then went over to pick up the book. There was no sense in taking out her feelings on inanimate objects. "No."

"There's a punching bag at the gym," Heather offered. "I can drive you."

"There're men at the gym," Brooke countered, "and right now, I don't know what I'd do if I ran into one of them."

A movement outside caught her eye, and Heather looked out the window. Speak of the devil. "Well, you'd better think fast because there's one coming up our front walk."

Moving back to the recliner, Brooke froze. She knew immediately. Something in Heather's voice gave it away. Tyler. "No."

"Yes."

She couldn't go through another scene like the one in his office. Flight was the only alternative. Brooke hurried to the hall. "I don't want to see him."

Heather was already on her way to the front door. "You take one step up those stairs, and so help me, Brooke, I'll throw you down." Heather pulled open the door before Tyler had a chance to ring the bell.

"Hello, Heather. Brooke." He felt awkward, being here. He felt even more awkward being home. Or anywhere else without her. Knowing he would continue to be without her if he didn't do something. It might be too late even now, but he had to try.

Brooke felt as if her legs had suddenly turned into tree trunks. Stiff, wooden, they refused to take her anywhere.

"Hi—" About to say "Tyler," Heather stopped herself, then let the greeting pass unattended. They'd work names out later. If there was a later. "Well, I'll just leave you two alone. I have homework to do."

Wedging herself past Brooke, who was still standing at the foot of the stairs, Heather raced up the rest of the way. Once in her room, she closed her door loudly to let them know they had the privacy they obviously needed.

Dammit, she still cared, Brooke thought. She should hate the sight of him for lying to her, for refusing to let her into his life, but she didn't. She still loved him. What kind of an idiot did that make her?

Knotting her fingers together, she tried to look impassive. "What are you doing here?"

This was good. She wasn't throwing him out. Tyler took a guarded step toward her, aware that she might bolt. That she'd cut him off before she heard him out. He'd thought long and hard about this, consulting no one but his conscience. And finally, last night, the girls. They understood far more than children their age should have. And like him, they missed having Brooke in their lives. "I came to talk."

Even as she looked at him, she was trying to seal herself off. "More stories?"

He took another step. Then another. Until he was standing next to her. "No, the truth."

Brooke raised her chin, her eyes challenging him. "How would I know?"

It was a gamble. He knew that. All or nothing, but he had no other options. Except to walk away from her, and he wasn't willing to do that. "You'll just have to trust me."

She pressed her lips together, afraid to risk it. More afraid not to because the alternative hadn't worked out for her. She couldn't do without him, no matter what she told herself or Heather.

The words were guarded. "Go ahead."

Instead of beginning, he took her hand and led her to the sofa in the living room. "What I'm about to tell you is going to sound more like a lie than anything you ever heard from your ex-husband. My name isn't Tyler Breckinridge."

He wasn't saying anything she didn't know, but to hear him admit it was at least gratifying. "You're Tom Conway, aren't you?"

"Yes."

"Then why deny it?" she asked.

He gave her an explanation she could readily understand. "Because Tom Conway has three daughters whose lives are in danger. Three daughters who could be gunned down just the way their mother was."

Her mouth fell open. She heard the words, but they were difficult to assimilate. "Gunned down? Why? By whom?"

The only way he could tell her was to distance himself from the memory. The one that still haunted him.

"I didn't realize it until it was too late that Gina, the vibrant sensitive woman I fell in love with, was the daughter of a prominent figure in a crime syndicate." A sad smile curved his mouth. "People don't come with disclaimers printed on their foreheads." And then he shook his head. "Probably wouldn't have mattered if they did. I would have fallen in love with her, anyway. Because of her, I could see beyond the confining structure of my disciplined life. I could see colors and appreciate the small things. Because of her I learned to feel again."

This was painful for him. But she had to know in order to understand. Brooke slipped her hand over his. "Why was she gunned down?"

"Her father ran into some kind of trouble with one of the other bosses. Retribution came on the heels of a warning that was only hours old." Tyler's jaw hardened. "First Gina's mother was killed to teach him his place, then Gina. I saw the whole thing. I was in the garage, fifteen feet away. They didn't see me. And I couldn't stop it.'' That was something that would always haunt him. That he hadn't been able to help, hadn't been able to protect her. ''The district attorney asked me to testify. I did.'' Two words. Two small words that in no way began to cover the hell he'd endured before the trial was finally over. Before those responsible were put away.

''Most of the people who could hurt the girls and me are either in prison or dead, but there's always a small chance.'' Tyler realized Brooke was holding his hand. He curled his fingers around hers. ''The government thought it best if the girls and I just disappeared one night. So we did.'' He looked at her. ''I would have stayed if it was only me, but there're the girls to think of. The witness protection program took care of everything. Gave us new identities, secured the position in the music department, bought the house, the furniture. Everything. We had to leave our own things behind.''

That explained a great deal. There was just one more piece that hadn't been fit in. ''Who was the woman who called asking for you?''

''Carla.'' Affection entered his eyes. ''My younger sister. She's the only family I have left, and I couldn't bear to leave her behind with no explanation, no word. I finally managed to call her from a public phone right outside Las Vegas. That was the first contact. We have a system. The last time we spoke, she told me she knew someone who could scramble the lines for us so the calls can't be traced in either direction.''

He took her hands in his. Now Brooke knew everything. ''I was hoping to eventually reclaim my old life after a few years. But now I don't want to.''

Suddenly, her breathing became arrested. ''Oh?''

''I don't want any life without you. These last two weeks have shown me that. After I lost Gina I didn't think I could ever love anyone again, other than the triplets and Carla.'' He paused, trying to read her expression. ''You realize that you can't tell anyone, not even Heather, about this? That my life and the girls' lives are all in your hands?''

She nodded solemnly. ''Yes, I realize that.'' It would be hard keeping this from Heather. But she'd manage. Heather knew when to back off.

''And that you also hold something else in your hand?''

''What?''

He turned her hand over so that her palm faced up. ''My heart.''

Her eyes smiled at him. ''I thought I felt something beating.''

It was time to get the rest of it out. ''If you're willing to put up with all this, willing to have a man who, according to records, is essentially only about four months old...''

Anticipation began to wind through her. ''Yes?''

This wasn't easy for him. Finding words never had been. That was one of the reasons he gravitated to music. He could express himself so much more easily that way. Maybe she'd understand what he was trying to ask if he played the "Wedding March" for her.

He looked around. "Where do you keep your piano?"

She took his hand, drawing his attention back to her. "No more obstacles between us. Just tell me."

He had faced down Gina's killers. This shouldn't have been that difficult for him. But it was. Matters of courage always were. "I love you, Brooke. Will you marry me?"

She'd begun to think he'd never say it. "Yes. Oh, yes." Brooke threw her arms around his neck. But just before he kissed her, she drew her head back. "And I love you—" She stopped abruptly. "What do I call you—Tom or Tyler?"

Names didn't matter. Only feelings did. "You can call me anything you want, as long as it's me you're calling."

"No problem," she told him just as his lips touched hers.

And there wasn't. Not any longer.

*　*　*　*　*

Watch for Marie Ferrarella's next books, HERO FOR HIRE, coming in June from Silhouette Sensation, AN ABUNDANCE OF BABIES from Silhouette Special Edition in April, and TALL, STRONG & COOL UNDER FIRE from Silhouette Desire in May.

AVAILABLE FROM 15TH MARCH 2002

AN ABUNDANCE OF BABIES Marie Ferrarella

That's My Baby!

Delivering Stephanie Yarbourough's babies in a car park was a unique way for Sebastian Caine to reintroduce himself to his old flame. And with Stephanie planning to raise the babies alone, he kept dropping by just to help…

THE MILLIONAIRE AND THE MUM
Patricia Kay

The Stockwells

Mercenary Jack Stockwell had a mission to find out if his family had swindled Beth Johnson's ancestors out of a fortune. The strong, earthy woman and her two children stirred feelings deep within him. But how would Beth feel when she discovered that her lover was actually a Stockwell?

A LOVE BEYOND WORDS Sherryl Woods

Vulnerable Allie Matthews preferred her life risk-free—until Ricky Wilder pulled her from the rubble of her home and coaxed her out of her cautious world. Could she trust her life to the sexy fire-fighter who lived his whole life on the edge?

THE MARRIAGE MAKER Christie Ridgway

Montana Brides

Ethan Redford proposed marriage—and motherhood—to Cleo Kincaid Monroe expecting a 'yes'. After all he knew being a bride and a mum to little Jonah was Cleo's dream. But Ethan's honour demanded that he must not take advantage of his virgin bride!

HIDDEN IN A HEARTBEAT Patricia McLinn

A Place Called Home

From the moment Rebecca Dahlgren stepped onto Far Hills Ranch, Luke Chandler was hard to miss, with his sexy broad chest and his sleepy eyes that weren't interested in sleeping. This 'strictly business' consultant knew she was about to get into trouble!

BABY OF CONVENIENCE Diana Whitney

Laura Michaels needed a powerful husband to keep custody of her son—and millionaire Royce Burton needed a wife. So they made a deal: marriage—for the baby's sake.

Fortune's Children

THE GROOMS

Welcome back to the drama and mystery of the Fortune dynasty

Fortune's Children: The Grooms—
five strong, sexy men
surrounded by intrigue, but
destined for love and marriage!

*The Fortune's Children legacy
continues in this popular continuity
series with two new books a month.*

Diana Palmer

THE TEXAS RANGER

He has a passion for justice

Published 15th March 2002

FREE
2 BOOKS
AND A SURPRISE GIFT!

We would like to take this opportunity to thank you for reading this Silhouette® book by offering you the chance to take TWO more specially selected titles from the Special Edition™ series absolutely FREE! We're also making this offer to introduce you to the benefits of the Reader Service™—

★ FREE home delivery   ★ FREE gifts and competitions
★ FREE monthly Newsletter   ★ Exclusive Reader Service discount
★ Books available before they're in the shops

Accepting these FREE books and gift places you under no obligation to buy; you may cancel at any time, even after receiving your free shipment. Simply complete your details below and return the entire page to the address below. *You don't even need a stamp!*

YES! Please send me 2 free Special Edition books and a surprise gift. I understand that unless you hear from me, I will receive 4 superb new titles every month for just £2.85 each, postage and packing free. I am under no obligation to purchase any books and may cancel my subscription at any time. The free books and gift will be mine to keep in any case.

E2ZEC

Ms/Mrs/Miss/Mr ....Initials................................
BLOCK CAPITALS PLEASE

Surname...

Address..

....

....Postcode ....

Send this whole page to:
UK: FREEPOST CN81, Croydon, CR9 3WZ
EIRE: PO Box 4546, Kilcock, County Kildare (stamp required)

Offer valid in UK and Eire only and not available to current Reader Service subscribers to this series. We reserve the right to refuse an application and applicants must be aged 18 years or over. Only one application per household. Terms and prices subject to change without notice. Offer expires 30th June 2002. As a result of this application, you may receive offers from other carefully selected companies. If you would prefer not to share in this opportunity please write to The Data Manager at the address above.

Silhouette® is a registered trademark used under licence.
Special Edition™ is being used as a trademark.